Fading Light

Also by Melissa Ann:

A Silent Canvas Series:
A Silent Canvas Part One
A Silent Canvas Part Two
A Silent Canvas Part Three

Unbound By His Love Series:
Unbound by His Love
Unbound by His Love 2
Unbound by His Love 3

Also by David S. Scott:

Igniting Passions
Santa's Son

The Phoenix Series:
Deep in You
Deeper in You

FATE ALWAYS WINS

DAVID S. SCOTT
& MELISSA ANN

By Melissa Ann and David S. Scott

Cover design by Darkmantle Designs

Printed in the United States of America

First Printing: January 2018

Published by Seraph Wing Publishing

ACKNOWLEDGEMENTS:

The authors would like to thank:

Jeff Walterhouse. Without you, this would have never been written. Thank you for that. Remember, everyone comes into our lives for a reason. Some are blessings. Others, to teach us a lesson. Take that as you will.

A special thanks to the very talented Darkmantle Designs for the *awesome* job on the cover and formatting.

To all the members of *David S. Scott's House of Smartassery*, we both appreciate everything you do.

To our sole Beta Reader—Marcia Mason-Heaston—thank you for everything you have done. This book wouldn't have been the same without you.

David would like to add,

To J.T. Lozano, for planting the co-writing idea in Melissa's head. I ended up having to put way more effort in than when I was just editing. I'll remember that. :P

To Melissa, thank you for allowing me to take part in this adventure with you. I know this book is truly filled with your blood, sweat, and tears. I've been honored to stand by your side as the story unfolded, and hope that you were pleased with my contributions to it. Here's to many more, my friend.

Last, but not least, we'd both like to give a huge *Thank You* to you, the reader. Without readers, there would be no reason for writers to write. I hope you enjoy *Fading Light* and consider leaving a review to let us and other readers know what you thought.

This book is dedicated to you, our readers.

And remember...

"It's' better to have loved and lost, than never to have loved at all."

FOREWORD BY MELISSA ANN

Fate. I believe in fate.

I believe that every decision we make–and every road we take–is fate at work. Whether the events are positive or negative, it will bring us closer to our intended outcome. Every relationship that has failed steers us into a new direction. We learn from our mistakes… or we don't. But with each experience a new path is formed. Eventually, we walk enough miles to bring us to what was meant to be.

I am thrilled that David agreed to write this book with me, because I truly believe that at a time I needed someone, he came into my life. He has been an incredible friend and if it wasn't for him, I am not sure I could have made it through a particularly difficult time in my life. Not in one piece.

Fading Light is a story about fate. You can fight it all you want…

…but fate always wins.

Table of Contents

PROLOGUE

I am your heart. I am your light. Let my love heal you.

I squinted at the flickering image of my X-screen, the words almost too blurry to decipher. My head pounded as the hangover demons wreaked havoc inside my brain. The constant *drip drip drip* of the sink made my pulse race. I dragged myself to my feet and went to shut it off. I rubbed my temples. What the hell had I been thinking?

Lukas.

He'd broken my heart. I didn't even know what I could have done wrong, but it was obvious that he'd chosen her over me… and that he had no intention of changing his mind. It was so unfair that one person could ruin someone else's life like that with no consequences.

The night before came back to me in disjointed pieces. Lukas, so cold and cruel. My broken-hearted walk home in the rain. The booze… oh, so much booze.

I'd wanted to beg him to take me back. To email him and plead my case. We'd been together for almost a year. How could he discard me like trash now?

But I knew I sounded pathetic, so I drank some more to dull the pain. Before I knew it, I couldn't even see my screen, much less email anyone.

No matter how much I tried, I couldn't remember anything further. What then was on my X-screen?

I shuffled back to my chair and glared at the tiny image once more. This wouldn't do. I lifted a shaking hand and flicked at the words that were cheerfully taunting me, allowing the X-screen to enlarge the images into a virtual reality filling my office.

Words… not mere gibberish, but a story. I must have decided to bleed some of my emotion out into a new book. Part of me was relieved; I hadn't written anything in months. The rest of me was shocked that I'd managed anything more complicated than nonsense words like *dzztv.*

Well… this should be interesting.

I admit I hadn't handled my heartache well, turning to alcohol to ease my torment. Writing had always been my outlet, and being trapped in a writing block has been like losing part of myself. Then… Lukas took another part of me with him when he dumped me. I was but a shell of what I once was.

But maybe… I read the words surrounding me, filling me with hope. Maybe this would reignite my drive to write, or at least to finish this manuscript.

I'd always plotted out my stories before writing them, but this time felt different. It felt like the words had a grip on my heart and the emotions wanted to flow through my fingertips and into the book like blood. Taking a deep breath, I surrendered and took the plunge.

Prologue

CHAPTER ONE

He was my soul mate. I'd known it from the moment our eyes had met on our first date. It had been years since we'd last seen each other, but I'd still recognized him at first glance. His familiarity was both comforting and exciting, in a way. Gone was the baby-faced boy I remembered from so long ago, but he'd aged well, becoming even more handsome than I'd once expected. There'd been no anxiety to tie me in knots about meeting him. Instead, his presence had washed over me, leaving a comfortable warmth in my very soul. I felt drawn to him, and he was drawn to me. His touch called to some deeper part of my soul, and I never wanted him to stop. Could this be fate working its magic? We'd both been through tough separations, and though our situations were very different, I could recognize my own pain reflected in his eyes. We both had walls that we'd built around our hearts, and it would be our love that would tear them down… brick by brick.

One date quickly became two, and two became three. Heavenly days turned to blissful weeks. We'd found ourselves at my place, intending to watch a movie. In the flickering light of the television, the etched lines of his face called to me, begging me to touch him. How could I resist? The warmth of his body, his scent, even the sound of his breathing sent my pulse into overdrive. Would it always be this way? He'd become my addiction, and I never wanted to be cured.

His lips softly kissed my neck and shoulder, setting my naked skin on fire everywhere he touched. I closed my eyes and let his love wash over me, humming my pleasure deep in my throat. Jesse hadn't been my first lover since my separation, but he stood out from all the others. He understood me. He could read my body like a book, could play it like a violin.

I wanted this to be quick and rough, but at the same time, I needed to savor it. Before Jesse, it had been a long time since anyone had truly worshipped my body. Too long. My breath caught in my throat as he worked his way down my stomach. His hands stroked my thighs and he nudged my legs apart with a gentleness that stole my breath away.

Jesse inhaled deeply. "You smell incredible. You're like a delicacy that I'll never get enough of."

I blushed. He made me feel so dirty, so wanton… yet so cherished. My eyes fluttered closed as his tongue ran the length of my drenched pussy lips, licking up the juices. I released my breath in a hiss, trying not to hyperventilate.

"Christ, Brooklyn, you're soaking wet for me."

"That feels so good."

"And you taste incredible. I could lick your sweet pussy for hours, for days." His tongue lapped at my sensitive clit once more.

"Jesse… like that. Please don't stop."

His mouth and tongue on me felt amazing, far better than anyone else I'd ever experienced. My hands grasped the sheets and I imagined a world where my day was spent being orally gratified by Jesse. And, though I could have lived an eternity at the mercy of his talented tongue, I needed him inside me. Now.

"Jesse…" My voice was breathy, needy. "I need you to fuck me. Right now. I have to feel you inside me."

Without hesitation, he climbed up my body and kissed me, a feral desperation in his eyes. I moaned at the taste of my own flavor on his lips. With one swift move, he plunged himself deep inside and froze, both of us crying out from the intensity. In my gut, I knew this wasn't random sex, a temporary fling to be cast aside as we grew tired of each other. Jesse was the *one*; he was my soulmate. With him, it all meant so much more. Our bodies and souls were connected as one… he was my home.

"I want your cock to be the last one inside me." I confessed.

"It will be." His whispered promise spoke to the deep recesses of my soul.

"You're so big. Oh my god, I love having your huge cock deep inside me." I purred, my breath whispering over his ear. Unable to resist the temptation, I nibbled hard on his delicious lobe. My hips moved up to meet him, my body welcoming him still further inside.

"God, you feel incredible. Like you were made in heaven for me, and only me. Get on your knees. I want to fuck you from behind." He flipped me onto my stomach, covering my back with his chest. Leaning close he rasped, "On your knees, Babe."

His palm slapped my ass as I lifted it into the air. He pressed his lips to each cheek before grabbing my hips and slamming his cock into me.

"Fuck!" My hair was swept off my back and wrapped around Jesse's hand. He tugged it back with each thrust, pushing himself deeper. I was fully under his control and I revelled in it, savored it. It hurt a little and my neck ached from his onslaught, but I loved it. His cock rammed into me, hitting that spot deep inside with perfect precision. My legs began to tremble as my climax neared.

"Don't stop! Don't ever stop," I gasped. My toes curled as pleasure deep inside me built to a crescendo. I gasped out a garbled version of his name as my orgasm exploded like fireworks, radiating outward, leaving me relaxed and sated.

"Brooklyn, oh God…" Jesse pumped into me twice more and froze, pressing himself deep inside me. My lips found his and I kissed him tenderly as I waited for him to come down from his orgasm. The fast beat of his heart comforted me.

"Will it always be like this?" I asked the question that had plagued me from the moment we'd reconnected.

Jesse grinned at me, and I could see the love in his eyes. "I hope so. Brooklyn… I lo–"

His phone rang, interrupting our tender moment. Jesse was always on call, so I knew he had no choice but to answer it.

"It's Melinda." His expression was a cross between annoyance and confusion. Melinda was his ex-wife.

He let out a rather loud sigh before answering. I decided to fetch myself a glass of water so he could have some privacy. Besides, our exertions had made me thirsty. As I got up from the bed Jesse shot me an apologetic look. I cupped his cheek and he leaned into my hand, only to snap upright at something Melinda said. I smiled at him reassuringly as I left the room. We both had a past and the accompanying baggage that came with it

Leaning against the counter, I stood with the glass resting against my chin, and thought about how quickly life could change. After I'd left my ex-husband, I was convinced I would never find someone who wanted to commit. There were plenty of people on those dating sites ready and willing to have sex, but didn't want the messy emotions that accompany real relationships. That wasn't me. Jesse had messaged me, and we'd hit it off right away. We had so many things in common, it made me wonder if fate was truly the driving force. To think… we had walked by each other in the hallways of a school we'd both hated, not knowing that our paths would merge together twenty years later.

"Hey, Babe." Jesse sauntered into the kitchen.

My heart sank. His clothes were on. His thumb toyed with his keyring and I knew he was preparing to say goodbye. My shoulders started to hunch but I shook it off, standing up straight and tall to flash him a wide grin. Whatever had happened must have been important for him to leave so suddenly. I'd have to let go of my disappointment. "Hey, Bad Boy. Was it so terrible that you can't wait to get out of here?"

Jesse's lip curved up on one side. "Not at all. I had a great time with you. Unfortunately, I have to cut it short. Melinda is concerned about Nicholas. I guess he has a high fever and she needs me to bring her some medicine."

Jesse took his role as a father extremely seriously. It's one of the things I loved about him. One day, maybe we would all become a family.

Were we moving too quickly? I mentally shook my head. It can't be wrong, not when it feels so right. In the beginning, my walls had stood tall, but his words had spoken to my heart and although I hesitated, bit by bit he's chipped away at my defenses.

"I understand, and I hope Nicholas is okay. Please call me when you get there, and buckle up!" I pressed my lips against Jesse's and smiled.

On our first date, I had teased him when I caught him not wearing his seatbelt. He'd merely shrugged off my concern and told me he hated the constricting feeling of wearing it.

"I will… call that is. I'm a good driver. Nothing will happen."

Nagging him about something he had obviously done a million times before was going to do nothing but annoy him or make him *want* to do the opposite of what I asked. My best friend was like that. I've learned that the most effective thing to do is grab a shot glass and some whiskey and have a drink. If there wasn't any liquor, then banging my head on the table worked too. *Ugh. Stubborn men.*

As he shoved his wallet into his back pocket a card fell onto the floor. I bent over to pick it up and noticed it was an emergency card. Jesse was diabetic, and it was imperative that he carry the card since he refused to wear a medic alert bracelet.

"I guess I should change my emergency contact. I've been meaning to take Melinda off, but life got busy and I forgot." He stammered over his words, his face a slight tinge of red.

"No worries. I know how busy you are." I gave him a reassuring smile and leaned forward for a kiss. It was true. Jesse was either at work or with me, and I certainly kept him occupied. It was no wonder that some of the little things were forgotten.

Chapter One

CHAPTER TWO

Fall brought cooler weather, and with it, nature's kaleidoscope of colors. The trees shed their greenery and displayed glorious shades of red, yellow, and orange. You could almost taste the pumpkin spice in the air. It had always been my favorite time of the year, but now I found myself resenting the cooler weather. The change in seasons meant Jesse had to work more for his landscaping job, clearing away fallen branches and leaves before they became hazards for drivers and pedestrians alike. I missed him during the long hours he was away. I tried to make the best of it, though.

Our very active sex life was great inspiration for the hot scenes in my book. We were compatible in the bedroom in so many ways. Neither of us ever shied away from trying new things in bed, and it was fun vying for who would take control. Each time we were together, it was a new experience, an adventure. Finding my sexual equal was both refreshing and liberating.

"I'm under your spell. I don't know what you've done to me, but I just can't stay away from you." His words spoke directly to my heart. Butterflies fluttered in my stomach; something I hadn't felt since I was a teenager. Things with Jesse felt like they were perfect, almost too good to be true. I was a little afraid to pinch myself for fear I'd wake up and find it had all been a dream. I knew I had a history of falling in love too quickly, though, so I was a little afraid of letting myself really relax and let him in. After everything I'd been through, what if I ended up jinxing things?

"If there's magic involved, I'm consumed by it, too. I feel the exact same way." Every waking minute, it seemed, my thoughts were on him. I'd remember how I felt when he'd hold me, when he kissed me. When I was alone, my thoughts traveled to his gentle touches and caresses when we'd make love. When we were apart, time couldn't seem to move fast enough until we could be back in each other's arms, and that thought was terrifying. I loved and I feared my body and mind's reactions to him. He made me vulnerable. He made me *hope.* We were headed for the kind of love you only see in romance novels, but I knew I was giving him the power to crush me if he chose. Love was always a risk, but the reward was worth it if you found the right one. I'd just never dared to dream that it could happen to me.

"When I get off work, I want to take you somewhere."

"Oh? Where are we going?"

"Hmm… well, I could tell you, but I think it would be more fun to surprise you."

I giggled. "Give me a hint?"

"Nope."

I stuck my lower lip out, though I knew he couldn't see it over the phone. "Come on! You have all this work stuff keeping you busy all day, but now I won't be able to write because I'll be crazy with curiosity."

"You know, you're adorable when you pout." I could hear his smile through the phone. "Bring a sweater. I have to go, Babe. See you soon."

Was it childish to jump for joy? It probably was, but I couldn't help it. It had been so long since anyone had made me feel like I was on cloud nine. Not even my ex-husband had ever been able to do that. I'd never been so happy, but deep down, that awful, nagging voice kept harping at me to be careful. I had it bad, I knew I should listen to my subconscious and scale it back, but I couldn't do it. My heart has always ruled over my head, and that was probably why I ended up hurt so much.

"See you soon, my Bad Boy. I'll be ready."

He chuckled. "See you soon."

The clock was broken, I was sure of it. I had been staring at it for the last six months, but it had only shifted by a couple of hours. I shook my head at myself. The euphoria I felt was like a drug. I needed my fix, though I knew I was acting like a silly, love-struck teenager.

Move, clock. Seriously. This is ridiculous.

"You ready to go, Babe?"

I jolted, squealing. "What the hell, Jesse? Have you been taking lessons from Damian in how to scare the shit out of me? How did you get in without me noticing?"

Jesse chuckled, his eyes crinkling. "No lessons needed from your best friend. You're just so easy. I do have to admit, though, *that* was funny. As for how, I used my key and walked in. It's not my fault you were sitting here, staring off into space."

"*Easy?* You think I'm easy?" I crossed my arms. "I am not!"

"You're still adorable when you pout. Hey..." Jesse pried my arms apart and pulled me into his embrace. "I don't think you're easy. I think you're sexy. And so desirable... Brooklyn, do you have any idea what I want to do to you right now?"

"Let's stay in then," I whispered, my fingers trailing toward his jeans.

He caught my straying fingers, brushing his lips against mine and sending tingles through my body. What was I angry about again? "Can't do that or you won't get to see your surprise. Get your purse. Let's go."

He released me, leaving me reeling. I sighed dramatically and picked up my sweater and my purse and followed him out the door. "You'd better be planning to wear your seatbelt this time, or so help me..." I muttered under my breath, knowing he wouldn't. He took pleasure in messing with me, and if I drew attention to it, he'd be *sure* to do the opposite of what I'd asked.

My surprise turned out to be a trip to a secluded lake. Jesse parked on the side of an old dirt road a few miles outside of town. I thought he'd lost his mind, but he only smiled and held out his hand to me in response to that playful question. Ten minutes later, we broke through the treeline to find an unspoiled meadow and, beyond that, a pristine lake, glittering in the late afternoon sunshine. Long grass and wildflowers filled the meadow, and I couldn't help but reach out to skim my fingers through it.

"Jesse, it's beautiful," I breathed. "How did you know this was even here?"

"A long time ago, like way back in high school, I used to explore these woods whenever I had a chance. Sometimes I felt like I needed to get away from everything, from my family, from the stress of school… all of it. This became my sanctuary. I've never shown it to anybody." He picked up a small stone and flung it into the lake, watching it skip across the water.

I gaped at him, completely blown away. “No one? Not even your ex-wife?”

He shook his head. “Melinda hates being outside. I didn’t think she’d like it.”

“It’s beautiful. I’m so touched, I–” I swallowed back the lump forming in my throat. He turned to look at me and I didn’t want him to see me cry over this, so I did the only thing I could think of. I launched myself at him, kissing him with every ounce of passion I had.

He caught me, lifting me up as though I weighed nothing. I wrapped my arms and legs around him, and nipped at his lower lip. I felt his cock growing, pressing so near to where I wanted it to be. I flexed my hips into him, relishing in the sound of his responding moan.

“I want to taste you, Jesse,” I whispered against his lips. “Here, by your lake.”

“Are you sure?”

“I’ve never been surer of anything in my entire life.”

Jesse set me down and I dropped to my knees, smiling up at him through my lashes. Without breaking eye contact, I lightly scratched my nails over his cock, still hidden beneath his clothing. It jerked at the contact and, feeling bold, I leaned forward and kissed him there.

"Do you believe in fate?" I asked.

"Yes, I do." The sun was beginning to set, turning the sky brilliant purple and pink colors. His eyes gleamed hungrily as he waited for me to do something. Slowly, methodically, I unbuttoned his jeans and lowered the zipper, releasing his trapped erection. His breath hissed out through his teeth as I stroked him, letting my hand come all the way up to tease the tip. "Right now, I'd believe in anything for you."

"Silly. I was asking you a serious question."

Sometimes I had trouble believing that Jesse and I had met in grade school. We were just innocent kids back then. How strange was it that this is where we'd end up so many years later. I couldn't help but wonder if it was fate that had brought us together as kids, and then led us back together now when the time was right. The idea was certainly over-romanticized and, perhaps, a little far-fetched… but it wasn't out of the realm of possibility.

"Now isn't the time for serious questions. Now is the time for your lips to be around my cock."

I chuckled and lightly licked the underside of his shaft, tracing the big vein that ran underneath. "So you want me to suck it, do you?"

"Mmm hmm," he panted. "Stop teasing me."

"Say it. Say what you want from me."

"Suck my cock, Babe. Please."

I loved sucking his dick almost as much as I loved teasing him. The way he moaned when I took him in my mouth set my pulse racing. Hollowing my cheeks, I sucked hard as I bobbed up and down. A small drop of pre-come squeezed out the tip, and I lapped it up greedily, moaning at the flavor of him on my tongue. I released his cock and gave him a wicked grin.

"Mmm. You taste good."

Jesse was watching me intently, a smile on his face. His hands found my head and he pushed, urging me back onto his dick. My tongue swirled around the tip of his cock before he slid back into my mouth. With a groan, he pushed me down further, encouraging me to take him deep.

"*Fuck.* That feels good." He rasped.

His cock hit the back of my throat, and I held him there, sucking and swallowing his length. His breathing had grown louder and more erratic, and I could feel him harden by the second. I moaned, knowing that not only the sound but the vibration from my voice would give him even more pleasure.

I slid my tongue up the side of his cock before releasing it once more.

"I want you to come, deep in my mouth, so I can taste you. Would you like that?" I asked teasingly.

"Ride me. I want to finish inside you." His voice sounded husky and full of need. I quickly removed my clothes, and he wasted no time plopping himself onto the ground, his cock standing proudly at attention.

I clambered on top of him and eased myself down, relishing the feel of him stretching me with delicious fullness. Being on top was one of my favorite positions. I mean, I loved everything we had tried, but being on top was the best of the best. I loved watching his face as he lost himself in my rhythm, plus I loved the friction I was able to achieve while riding him. I pumped my hips, picking up speed. My eyes flew to his as he caught my breasts in his hands, supporting them from their wild bouncing, squeezing them, kneading them. Before long, I felt that telltale tingle in my core that could only signal an imminent orgasm.

"Fuck, don't stop. That feels so good. Ride my cock, Babe." Jesse's hands moved to rest on my hips and pushed me further down his length, so that he filled me completely.

I leaned down and moaned in his right ear, before I feasted on his sensitive lobe and neck. I knew that would drive him wild. It always did.

"I'm close, so close. I need you to come with me." I was out of breath, but somehow managed to relay my message. "Oh God, I'm going to come! Come with me now!"

My body erupted, the relaxing warmth spreading throughout my body.

Jesse's moans merged with my own as he joined me, his cock twitching inside me as he came, each pulse feeling like small thrusts deep inside me.

I collapsed to his side, once again admiring the fading light of the sunset. Jesse wrapped his arm around me, pulling my head down to his smooth chest and shielding me from the ground. My fingers traced patterns over his jawline and throat as we caught our breaths.

"I love sex with you. It feels… special. And afterward, I always feel so relaxed; like you sucked all the stress out of me." Jesse was running his fingers along my shoulder. Neither of us, it seemed, could get enough of touching each other.

"So, I'm like your stress ball?" I giggled.

He snorted. "Well, I am not sure I would have used the word ball."

Jesse's phone pinged, and he sighed. "What do they need from me at work now?"

He yanked up his pants so he could reach his phone in his pocket. Tapping the screen, he growled.

"Looks like I have to go. Melinda says she blew a tire, and Nicholas is with her." He jumped to his feet and held out a hand to help me up. "I'll drop you off at home on the way."

"Isn't there someone closer who could help her? You have to drop me off, then drive all the way there. That means she'll have to wait on the side of the road until you arrive." What I really wanted to say was she needed to back off, but I knew that wouldn't go over well. I wished he could see what she was doing. Melinda was refusing to let him go and coincidentally she always needed help when we were together. She probably slashed her own tire just to spite me.

"It won't take me too long. I'm sorry I have to run out on you again." He was sincere. His eyes looked at me apologetically. I was getting used to seeing that look.

"No worries. We have the rest of our lives together."

"I love you, Babe. Thank you for understanding." Jesse leaned down and kissed me on the cheek. *On the cheek?* She *calls and now I'm relegated to being kissed on the cheek?*

Grrr. It was so frustrating. Melinda knew how to manipulate Jesse. He was a white knight, always there to rescue the damsel in distress… and she played her part well.

Chapter Two

CHAPTER THREE

"Hey Babe." He may have only been a voice on my phone, but I could tell he was smiling. It was nice knowing that I could affect someone that way.

"How's my Bad Boy?" I replied with an equally large grin.

He chuckled. "You mean Master Bad Boy."

"Yeah, whatever. You wish." Jesse had bested me at scrabble a few nights before. Again. For the umpteenth time. And he'd been bragging ever since. Honestly, the man was insufferable. It was a good thing I loved him or I'd have to strangle him.

"If you're going to pout, do it where I can enjoy the view at least."

"I'm not!" I sucked in my lower lip, upon realizing that I had in fact been pouting.

"Uh huh." From the tone of his response, it was obvious he didn't believe me.

"Are you on your way? *Master?*"

"Oh, say it again."

I let out an exaggerated sigh. "*Master.*"

"I love you and yes I am. Should be there in a half hour. I'm famished. I was running late and had to skip breakfast this morning. *Someone* kept me up late last night so I overslept. Speaking of which… I would rather be eating something else besides food for lunch."

"Mmm… me too. But you shouldn't be skipping meals whether that meal is me or *actual* food. Wouldn't want you passing out on me, especially during our extracurricular activities."

"Don't worry. I have some Starburst in the truck in case my blood sugar drops, but it's only thirty minutes; I should be fine."

"Okay. See you soon. Love you."

We were meeting at our favorite restaurant, Texas Roadhouse. I felt it was the perfect place to give him the news. It wasn't time for me to leave for the restaurant yet, so I spent that time pacing my living room floor willing the time to go quicker. *You should never wish your life away.* Those words danced in my head and it rang true, but it was so difficult to not want the clock to skip ahead.

I had arrived before Jesse, but for once they weren't busy. Normally, they made you wait until your entire party arrived before they'd give you a table, but the hostess recognized me and sat me right away. The table was near a window, so I occupied my time watching the cars in the parking lot.

The box that contained Jesse's gift was neatly wrapped in shiny silver paper and nestled in the side pocket of my purse. I still hadn't decided when to present it to him. The ideal time would be *after* we had eaten, but patience was *not* my forte. Also, I didn't know what his reaction would be to my gift. *Ugh,* my stomach hurt from the stress of not knowing... or perhaps I was just hungry.

I frowned at my phone. Jesse should have been here already. It was fifteen minutes after he said he'd be here. It was unlike him to be late to anything.

I'm sure he'll be here any minute.

The waitress came by to check on me, so I went ahead and ordered an appetizer. I called Jesse a few times to see where he was, but he didn't answer. While annoying, that didn't necessarily mean anything. I knew he tried to avoid being on the phone while driving if he could help it. He pretty much only answered work calls while in the car, and that was because he had to when he was on call. The man didn't like wearing his seat belt, but he considered being on the phone unsafe.

I stared at the plate of fried pickles, the delicious scent teasing me and making my mouth water. Ten more minutes passed and I caved. Surely Jesse wouldn't be angry if I had *just one* of them while I waited for him. He *was* late, after all. *Where on Earth could he be?*

I was on the very last pickle when my phone rang. I answered it without looking at the caller ID.

"Where have you been? Are you okay?" My words rushed out in a frantic jumble, betraying my worry.

"At work," The deep voice that answered wasn't Jesse. Damian, my best friend, sounded a little anxious. I frowned. He normally sounded calm, no matter what was going on. My pulse spiked as he continued. "You know, *some* of us have to do real work for a living. But never mind all that. You need to come to the hospital right now. Jesse has been admitted."

My heart jumped like it had been hit by an electrical shock. An immense weight settled in my chest, making it difficult to breathe. *Focus, Brooklyn.* Damian had said I needed to get to the hospital, so that must mean that Jesse was still alive.

"What happened? Is he all right?" My voice was high pitched and scratchy, not that I could hear myself over the loud ringing that had begun in my ears. I willed myself to calm down so I could hear Damian, but my body didn't want to cooperate.

"Brooklyn… did you hear me? He was in a car accident. I just finished taking his blood. He's being examined at this very moment, so I don't know the extent of his injuries. I told them at work I wasn't feeling well, so I'm already in the car. I'll come get you, you shouldn't be driving." He paused. Tell me where you are." His voice seemed so far away, like he was talking to me from the other side of a tunnel… but I did manage to hear what he said.

I shook my head, even though I knew he couldn't hear me. There was no way I could wait for him until he got here. Jesse needed me *now*. Besides, my imagination was running away with me, picturing all the worst-case scenarios. "I'll be fine. I'm leaving now."

"Brooklyn. I'm telling you, don't you dare get in that car…" Damian's voice was cut off as I hit the disconnect button. He knew me so well, but I couldn't deal with one of his lectures right now, I needed to get to Jesse.

CHAPTER FOUR

"I'm here to see Jesse Carson. He has been in an accident. I need to see him… please!" The run from the other end of the parking lot had left me breathless and red faced.

"Okay. Calm down, ma'am. What was that name again?"

How could she tell me to calm down? I didn't know how badly Jesse was hurt. He most likely wasn't wearing his seat belt. He could be dying, and so help me if I missed seeing him because this woman wanted me to calm down. I took a deep breath and tried not to shout.

"Jesse Carson. Please hurry. *Please* tell me he's okay." My sentence started off calm, but by the end I was in hysterics again.

The nurse tapped a few buttons on her keyboard and I wondered if they were required to have a certain level of typing skills because I felt like her fingers were moving in slow motion. *Ahh!*

"I cannot provide any information about his condition, and his chart has been marked as private. I cannot allow you to see him."

I must have misheard that. Perhaps it was the ringing in my ears again. "What?"

"I said I can't give you any information regarding Mr. Carson. His wife has declared that only immediate family is allowed into his room. That is… unless you are family?" She looked at me over her glasses, furiously clicking the pen that had appeared in her hand as if by magic.

What the fuck? I could feel the heat rise up my neck. My hands shook as I ran them through my hair. "Of course I am family. I am his girlfriend." *Surely, they would let me see him.*

Her eyes hardened as soon as I said the word "girlfriend." She put her pen down. "His *wife* said family, only." Her arms crossed firmly along her chest, suggesting that this discussion was closed.

"*Please!*" I didn't care how sad and pathetic I sounded, I would get down on my hands and knees if I had to. I needed to make sure that Jesse was okay.

"Not my call. I can't help you. Now, I'm afraid I'm going to have to ask you to leave. If you won't, I'll have to call security."

"Can't you at least tell me if he's okay?" I begged, the tears pouring down my cheeks, unchecked. "She's not even his wife, she's his ex-wife. Please, won't you help me?"

Her face softened as she placed her hand over mine. "She says she's his wife, and his medical identification card backs up her claim. Listen, there's nothing I can do. Rules are rules, but I will let them know that you were here, and I am sure that the family will contact you as soon as they can."

My voice wavered when I thanked the nurse. I knew it wasn't her fault, she was just doing her job… but I still resented her for it. Her, and that evil, nasty ex-wife of his, Melinda. The devil incarnate. How I would love to rip her arms out of their sockets and beat her to death with them. I sighed. Guilt weighed heavily on my heart. Now was not the time to fight with Melinda. She and everyone else close to Jesse were already dealing with a lot. My heart hurt to think about what his son Nicholas was going through.

Dejected, I left the hospital, realizing that the nurse never took my name. There was no point in going back. Even if she relayed the message, Melinda would never call me to update me on Jesse's condition. The soles of my shoes made a scratching sound in the leaves as I shuffled my way to the car. I was angry at Jesse for being stubborn and not putting his seatbelt on like I've asked. It had become a game to him to see how angry he could get me. It had never been a game to me. I just wanted to grow old with him. Was that too much to ask? I didn't think so. He was selfish for only thinking of himself and not the people he would leave behind. *Why wouldn t he listen to me?*

Ugh. I silently reprimanded myself for thinking that way. Right now, I needed to focus on sending positive vibes for his recovery. In the meantime, what was I going to do? The thought of sitting around in my condo without knowing what was going on horrified me. My arms wrapped around my stomach and I leaned over, resting my head on the cool steering wheel. The knot in my stomach tightened and I felt almost nauseous. Everything was out of control. It often was, really… in the past my parents, friends, and especially my ex-husband had thought I was weak and they had all tried to control my life. Everything was a mess now and there was *nothing* I could do about it. The accident, not being able to see Jesse, having to deal with his meddling ex-wife… all of it was out of my control. It was all too much.

Thud. My hands stung as I slammed them on the steering wheel, but I welcomed the pain. At least it was something I had done, something no one else had engineered. The pain was mine to control.

"Fuck!" I screamed, smacking the steering wheel a few more times for good measure. I jabbed at the radio and Linkin Park blared from the speakers. *Perfect.* They were my go-to band when I felt like throat-punching life.

"Fuck! Fuck! *Fuck!*" The last expletive was drawn out in a screech. Something moved in my peripheral vision and I turned to see people getting into the car parked next to me, staring through my window with something akin to horror. Without a word, they got in the car and fiddled with the panel on the inside of the door. Probably locking it from fear of being attacked by the crazy lady next to them. It was probably safe to say that I shouldn't be driving at all but I couldn't stay in the hospital parking lot forever.

I threw the car into gear and drove without a clear destination in mind, just needing to get *away* from there. Closest place I could think of was Damian's. Hopefully he went home… and wouldn't be too angry at me for hanging up on him. On second thought, maybe it would be better if he wasn't home.

I pulled into his driveway and sat in my vehicle for a good fifteen minutes, staring at nothingness. I was too spent to even think.

Tap. Tap. Tap.

"Jesus Christ!" I screamed and clutched my chest, glaring at the intruder to my solitude. Were this a cartoon, I'd be dangling comically from a chandelier. And life wouldn't suck so much right now, either. Cartoon characters had it easy. I shoved the door open and crossed my arms. *Ugh.* Damian was such an ass. Always trying to sneak up on me, and often succeeding. I found myself both irritated and relieved by his presence.

Damian held his belly as he laughed at my expense. *Jerk.*

"Serves you right for stalking me. By the way, why have you been sitting in my driveway staring at my house? It's creepy. *Creeper.*"

With Herculean effort, I mustered a sad, pathetic excuse for a smile. Damian's grin disappeared, and his eyes softened.

"Come here." He held out his arms and I wasted no time in cuddling close to his side. The tears flowed, the sobs making it impossible for me to speak. Damian just continued to hold me, telling me that everything would be all right. "I'm so sorry I couldn't be with you in the hospital, but with that Hitlerish woman making demands of everyone, I could have been fired for telling you he was even there. I had to clear out before anyone could see us together. I thought feigning illness so I could pick you up would be the best course of action. I should have stayed and waited for you..."

"No, you shouldn't have. I know this isn't your fault. They wouldn't let me see him anyway." I mumbled. I knew that Damian would be there in a heartbeat under other circumstances.

Suddenly, pins and needles covered my entire body, and I felt much too hot. I swallowed hard, fighting the nausea, unable to cry any longer. Damian took me by the hand and led me into his house. Within seconds, he'd surrounded me with a large assortment of donuts and ice cream. After all these years, he'd clearly learned that the best way to cheer me up was with sweets. He reached into his fridge and pulled out a bottle of wine. He nodded his chin in my direction, but I shook my head.

"Since when do you refuse alcohol when you're sad?" Damian looked at me suspiciously. I have dozens of selfies of him with that same expression. He will often send them at random times to keep me paranoid.

"I'm trying this new thing called self-control."

"Hmm." His gray eyes watched me as I stuffed another donut into my mouth, which was quickly followed by a spoonful of ice cream.

"Baby steps." I mumble. "Stop judging. Do you have any Cadbury crème eggs?"

"God, no. You know you aren't allowed to have chocolate when you're emotional. You'll just end up weepy. Well, weepi*er*. I can't and won't handle *that.* As for the donuts, I'm not judging. I've told you before that you need to put some meat on your bones. So, Miss Baby Steps, why aren't you with Jesse? I was going to text you and ask about him, but I figured I'd just wait for you to tell me." All traces of amusement were gone from his face. "What gives with Madam Stalin? I thought you told me they were divorced?"

"They are. She's Jesse's *ex*-wife, but she failed to mention the 'ex' part. Now she's refusing to let anyone but family see him, probably for the sole purpose of keeping *me* out." I rubbed at my temples, trying to stave off the headache I knew was coming on.

"How'd she even find out?"

"*Ugh.* He'd had her listed as his emergency contact for emergencies. He had meant to change that and hadn't gotten around to it yet, I guess." My words had come out a little harsher than I had intended. *Damn him for procrastinating.* A thought occurred to me. "Damian… how was he when you saw him?"

My best friend refused to meet my gaze. "Alive."

My face fell, as did my stomach. Maybe those donuts weren't such a good idea. "What aren't you telling me?"

"I don't know much. He was an unconscious, bloody mess. Despite all that, he seemed stable. People weren't panicking or calling codes or anything. Look, I wish I was in the position to get you in there to see him, but I'm only a phlebotomist. For what it's worth, though… I am kind of shocked that you let something like a stupid rule stop you from seeing him. The hospital doesn't keep close tabs on that stuff, so unless security is called, no one would think to stop you. They wouldn't realize you weren't supposed to be there. Where is that spitfire I know? This defeatist stranger eating sweets isn't *you.*"

"You're right," I said with a sigh. "You know how I let my emotions get the best of me. That nurse kept looking at me like I was some sort of *homewrecker*, and she wouldn't even tell me if he was okay. It was so frustrating and she pissed me off. Damian… he *has* to be okay. I don't know how I will go on if he isn't."

Damian handed me a tissue, which I bunched in my hand before wiping my nose with it.

"Let me see what I can do." Damian grabbed his phone and started to tap a number on his screen. He opened his patio door and stepped outside. He was probably going to use his charm to get some information on Jesse's condition. In the meantime, I'd go ahead and eat another donut, even though my stomach felt like it was ready to explode.

The patio door slid open and I turned toward Damian to assess his expression, but as usual, his stoic calm thwarted my attempts to read him.

"Okay. It looks as though Jesse's blood sugar was pretty low. That could be what caused him to run off the road and into a tree. On top of that, the airbag didn't deploy. It seems he hit the side of his head on something because the CT showed some swelling on his brain, so they need to keep him in a medically induced coma for a few days. He wasn't wearing his seatbelt, Brooklyn. He's lucky he's still alive." Even in my stressed-out state of shock, I could hear the disapproval dripping from his voice, no matter how professional he was trying to sound. That was my best friend for you, always judging… but he couldn't help it. I knew it was because he cared deeply about how people's decisions affected me.

Unfortunately, all my frazzled brain could grasp was that Jesse was in a coma. "Oh my god! What does that mean for him? Is he… is he going to be okay?" My chest heaved as I gasped for air. I couldn't breathe. The room was spinning, and the edge of my vision was starting to turn dark. A strong hand pushed my head down between my legs.

"Breathe, Brooklyn. In through your nose and out through your mouth. You are going to be fine." My body shook with silent sobs, tears streaming down my face as I fought for control. "Now, when you are done hyperventilating I will give you the rest of the news."

How did I ever survive without Damian? His was the cool head in this friendship; the rational one. I nodded, following his instructions. Soon, the floor no longer tilted, and I risked sitting up.

"Okay, you may continue." My hands were clenching and unclenching in my hands, a sign that I was barely keeping it together.

"You sure?" Damian looked from my hands to my eyes, his brow arched to emphasize his question.

"Yes, I'm sure!"

His hands went up in surrender before he continued. "As I was saying… he hit a tree, but it wasn't at an excessive speed, so his injuries could have been worse, and without the seatbelt, he could have been thrown from the vehicle. I wish I could tell you with certainty that he will make it through this, but with the swelling in the brain, it could go either way."

"Goddamn him! I have asked him time and time again to wear his seatbelt, but he acted like he was Superman, and invincible. Now, I may not get to have him in my life because he was a stubborn *ass*." My fist slammed on the kitchen table to emphasize my point. Anger felt good right now. *If he dies, it's all his fault. If he had only worn his fucking seatbelt he wouldn't be in this fucking mess.*

"Hey, my table is innocent in all this."

"Sorry. It's just unfair." I sniffed.

“Life’s unfair. You know that.”

Now *that* was an understatement. Guilt clawed its way into my heart, gripping it and adding even more weight to the heaviness that already sat there. Guilt… and sadness, anxiety, anger, and…was that *relief* I felt? Sure, I was beyond thrilled that he was alive but, in a way, I was almost grateful he was unconscious. A small, niggling fear had worried that he had known his ex had decided to exclude me. That maybe he’d chosen her over me when the chips were down. Now I knew he’d had nothing to do with it. Now that I thought about it, I’d be willing to bet that had been her plan all along. I’d always suspected she hadn’t been thrilled with me being in Jesse’s life.

“Now what? I go home and wait? Hope that he wakes up? Hope that he calls me?” I rubbed my stomach. This whole situation was making me feel ill. Too many emotions vied for dominance and twisted me in every direction.

“No.” Damian sighed. “What have I been saying to you? Do you even listen to me? You are going to get in your car and drive to the hospital and barge right into that room. Stop letting people push you around. You have every right to be there, kiddo." Damian's hand ruffled my hair. I couldn't help but giggle a little, despite my world crashing around me. Damian was younger than me but acted like an older brother. He was like my superhero, always there to protect me and wanting to fix everything.

"You're right." Before standing up, I grabbed another donut. "For the road." I held it up for Damian to see.

He snorted. "Well, it *is* a long drive. Go on, get out of here. He's in ICU, room 273, but you didn't hear that from me."

With the donut hanging halfway out of my mouth, I grabbed my purse and trotted out the door.

Chapter Four

CHAPTER FIVE

The drive back was less than ten minutes. I felt much better about seeing Jesse after talking to Damian. He had a way of calming me down. I was no longer contemplating murder, but my heart still ached. Jesse and I had spent every spare moment we'd had together since that first date. Being separated, unable to speak with him on the phone, made me miss him terribly. Half of myself was gone, and I hated the feeling of being unbalanced that it brought.

The gift I'd planned to give Jesse still sat on the passenger seat where I had thrown it earlier, its happy silver wrapping paper mocking me somehow. I'd pulled it from my purse so I could locate my keys quickly in my haste to get to the hospital. What if I never got the chance to give it to him? This was all his fault. Why couldn't he be bothered to spend less than a second fastening a seat belt? Why had he skipped breakfast to begin with? He *knew* better. For the second time today, I slapped my hand against the steering wheel. Maybe I should invest in a punching bag, so I could take all my aggression out on it.

My return to the hospital made my anxiety return in full force. I was relieved to see that there was a different nurse at the desk. This time I walked by as casually as possible in hopes I wouldn't draw any attention. It took everything I had to not run to Jesse's room. Patience was not a virtue I possessed. My heart hammered in my chest when I finally found it, so I paused to take a deep breath. Summoning all my courage, I stepped through the doorway. My eyes narrowed. Stalin, as Damian had called her, perched on the chair next to Jesse, holding his hand. A sudden inferno of searing heat raced along my skin and all I wanted to do was remove her hand from his. Forcibly. He was mine. Not hers. His hands, body, mind, love, everything…*mine. Maybe I could throat punch her*. My fists clenched as I fought against the burning need to pull her red hair like a grade school kid, but, instead, I counted to ten and managed to have some restraint.

Jesse lay there, still, silent. Blissfully unaware of the scene that was about to unfold right next to him. His face was pale except for the bruising caused from the collision. Monitors, IV's and all sorts of gadgets were hooked up to him. He looked so helpless and vulnerable… and it forced me to realize that every day was a gift and we should never take life for granted. *Did I tell him I loved him recently?*

"What are *you* doing here? I thought I had made it clear… family only." She rose to her full height, her green eyes never leaving mine. I wasn't about to back down, so I met her gaze, refusing to be the first to look away. My nails stabbed into my palms as I prepared to face Jesse's evil ex. If she wanted a confrontation, I'd give her one.

"I *am* his family, whether you like it or not. You will never keep me away from him. This isn't what he would want, and you know it. If you have *ever* loved him, then you should want to see him happy."

"He doesn't know what he wants. We spent most of our adult lives together. We have a child and I'm going to remind him of all the good times we had. This is just a phase; some sort of crisis. Soon enough, Jesse will forget all about you!" She sneered. "We'll be a family again, and our family has no room in it for trash like *you*."

"Trash? Melinda, call me what you like but no matter how you look at it, he gave *you* up and chose *me*. If I'm trash, what does that make you? Do your worst, bitch." The words sounded confident to my ears, but in my heart, I was afraid. Jesse didn't give his heart to many and when he did, he didn't give up easily. I could only hope that he knew that I would treasure his heart forever.

"Get out!" Melinda was pointing at the door with her manicured fingernail.

I've spent my entire life around people who have tried to control me, so it was unwise of her to think she could do the same. It only made me dig in my heels to do the exact opposite.

"I will not!" I shouted.

"Whoa, Ladies. I think we all need to simmer down a little. Mr. Carson doesn't need all this stimulation to his brain. He needs to be relaxed and in a soothing environment, so he can heal. Take it outside." A man with green scrubs and a stethoscope around his neck stood at the doorway. His voice may have been calm, but you could clearly see the annoyance on his face.

He was right. Coming here had been a bad idea. I knew there would be words between Melinda and I. It was selfish of me, and if this prolonged his healing process, I would never forgive myself. I cupped Jesse's face and stroked his cheeks gently.

I leaned down and whispered in his ear, "I am your heart. I am your light. Let my love heal you."

I turned and exited the room, but not before I saw the smile of victory on Melinda's face.

I flung my keys to the side, sighing in annoyance as I overshot my mark and they slipped into the crack between the table and the wall. Whatever. I'd get them later. I paused, listening to the sounds of my condo… or rather, the lack thereof. No one was here; no one was coming to be with me. Alone, once again. I knew I needed to stop feeling sorry for myself. Jesse was lying in a hospital bed, unconscious. When he awoke, would he wonder why I wasn't there? Would he think that I didn't care enough to stay with him? These new thoughts were like poison, working their way through my bloodstream and I felt ill, once again, only this time I threw up every bit of donut I had eaten, barely making it to the sink in time. *Yuck!* Donuts tasted much better going down than coming back up.

That did it. Today sucked and I just wanted to hide under my covers and pretend it never happened. It was a little early for my usual bedtime, but I wanted to block everything in my broken life out.

Climbing into bed, I stroked the cold sheets beside me. Jesse normally warmed that side of the bed. He was like my own personal heater. I pressed my nose into his pillow and I could still smell his musky cologne. Rolling onto my back, I stared at the ceiling, tears spilling from the corner of my eyes. *Please, bring him back to me.*

Time crawled, each second stretching to last years at a time. I drifted in and out of sleep, waking only to cry and cling once more to his pillow.

It was dark when I felt him, the bed dipping as he sat next to me and stroked my hair. "Hey, Babe. Why are you crying?"

"Jesse…" I curled around him, afraid to let go. "I didn't expect you so soon. I was so scared for you, scared for us."

"Shh… don't cry. Everything is going to be fine. I'm here. I'm here."

"I have so much I wanted to tell you, and I was terrified I'd never see you again." I hiccupped, trying to breathe around my sobs, my sadness tempered by my relief. "Jesse, I–"

He silenced me with a kiss, his lips melding perfectly to mine, as they always did. "I know, Brooklyn. I already know… and I feel the same. Kiss me. I need you. I can't stay long, but I needed to see you. Please…"

"Where are you–"

His kiss silenced me once more. He dragged me to him, running his hands all over my arms and back. Goosebumps rose everywhere he touched me, and I moaned out my pleasure. His tongue danced with mine, taking what he wanted but giving me so much more.

Jesse unzipped his jeans and pulled out his cock, wasting no time to climb on top of me and plunge himself inside me. My eyes welled with tears once more, the joy and love I felt escaping the only way they could—through my eyes. Normally, we had way more foreplay than this, but I understood. After his near-death experience, he wanted to reconnect as fast as possible. I couldn't have agreed more.

His thrusts sped, both in speed and intensity. I wrapped my arms and legs around him and kissed him everywhere I could reach. I laved sloppy kisses all over his chest, his shoulders, his neck. Jesse moaned, taking my mouth with his once more, drinking me in with the desperation of a man dying of thirst.

"I love you, Jesse…"

I pulled his face closer to mine, feeling his warm breath on my face. He didn't answer me, didn't say it back. I clawed at his back with my nails and said, louder, "I love you."

I awoke with a gasp, half sitting up, half rolling over. Jesse wasn't here. Of course he was still in the hospital. How could I be so stupid as to believe a desperate dream? He'd never been here… and I didn't know how I could stand being here by myself anymore.

I'd never felt more alone in my entire life.

CHAPTER SIX

As promised, Damian had been diligent with giving me as many updates as he could. Jesse had woken up and was finally leaving after being there for more than two weeks. I'd heard nothing from Jesse, himself. Damian had wanted to tell him to call me, but I told him not to. I'd texted a few times, but he'd never responded. I wanted Jesse to call on his own and *not* because Damian asked him. The fact that he hadn't even once made an effort to reach me, quite frankly, stung. Perhaps once he got settled in at home, he would call me. It was possible that Melinda's presence had made it difficult for him to contact me. With renewed hope, I picked up all the empty Twinkie wrappers that surrounded my spot on the couch.

"Hey." Damian's booming voice echoed through my empty apartment. He had startled me yet again, and I shrieked in response.

His laughter had always been a pleasant sound, even if it was at my expense. As usual.

"Jesus, Damian. How many times have I told you *not* to sneak up on me?" My hand was pressed against my chest, and I could feel my heart beating furiously.

"About a million… and when will you learn that I don't listen?"

"I guess I believe that there is hope for you to be a normal person."

He grasped his chest, mockingly. "You wound me. And anyway, you should just accept that I will never change. I'm constant, like a river. Or like having to pay bills."

"Uh-huh. And don't you ever knock?"

"Don't you ever lock the door? I could have been anyone, you know."

"*Ugh*, stop. I thought I did lock it. My head has been elsewhere lately. Cut me some slack. Anyway, you obviously came here to harass me for *some* reason… so what do you want?" My voice was edged with annoyance, but Damian knew I was just playing around.

"Checking up on you. I haven't seen you since, you know, *that* day. You tend to close yourself off from everything and everyone when you are sad." His gray eyes grew soft and his smile disappeared. He was right, I'd been avoiding human interaction as much as possible. It was simply too exhausting to pretend that everything was fine.

"I'm alive, and eating a ton of junk food." There was another Twinkie wrapper that was peeking out from under the couch. When depressed, I was either an emotional eater or I would lose my appetite completely.

Damian spotted me struggling with the empty wrapper and shook his head. "Well, like I told you, you need some more meat on your bones. I think this extra weight looks good on you, and your tits are bigger. Jesse will like that." He winked.

"Are you saying I am fat? And why are you looking at my… my… ti–boobs?" I shrieked as I crossed my arms over my chest, scandalized. I knew he was trying to get a reaction out of me and it had worked. The room felt warm from the ferocity of my blush. Damn him.

"Because I'm married, not dead. They're impossible not to notice. In fact, *noticing* is in my DNA." Damian hesitated. "So… when are you going to call Jesse?"

"I am waiting for him to call me." I knew I sounded impossibly stubborn, and I didn't care. I was right.

"But why? You're both adults here. Maybe he's waiting for *you* to call *him*. Someone has to be the grown up." *Ugh,* why does he always have to be so rational?

"I'm afraid of his reaction if I call. What if it's disappointment?" I restacked the magazines that had been sitting on my table. I couldn't bear to face him… what if I started crying again?

"But what if it isn't? What if it's relief? What if that one phone call is all it takes to continue your journey together?" He placed his hand over mine to stop me from fiddling with everything within reach.

"Okay, fine." I sighed.

Damian handed me my phone and plopped himself down on the couch, grabbing a magazine.

"Um… I'm not going to call him with you here."

"Why not?"

"Because that's awkward. Why would you even want to be here?"

"Just in case."

"In case *what,* exactly?"

"In case you chicken out, or in case you need me."

I rolled my eyes at him and huffed off into my bedroom, shutting the door behind me. I stared at my phone as though I'd never seen it before. My hands shook, and I had to redial a couple of times before I got it right. I couldn't be sure if I was more excited or nervous to hear his voice once more.

"Hi, Brooklyn." He almost sounded robotic. My heart sank. What happened to *Babe?*

"Hi. How are you feeling? I've missed you." My voice cracked, and I knew I was on the verge of tears. I struggled to fight back the lump forming in my throat, cutting off my airway.

"Sore and a bit slow. Melinda has been helping me out." His words lacked warmth and my heart ached. *I* should be the one helping him, not Melinda.

"I could have helped you. I still can, if…if you want me to."

He paused several seconds before answering. "Listen… these past few weeks have stirred up some feelings and memories. I thought I was over Melinda, but I've been thinking a lot about our time together. I don't think it is fair to you if I am dwelling on another woman while we're together." He sounded so cold. Distant. Did all our time together mean nothing to him?

"I don't even know what to say. You are making this decision for the both of us? I don't even get to have a say?" My voice sounded desperate, like I was clinging to a raft for dear life.

"Just remember you are a wonderful person and I will miss you."

"How can you say that to me when you don't want me? What does that even mean to you? Melinda is playing you. She threw me out of your hospital room and told me she was going to steal you away from me. I trusted you, I *loved* you… but you're *letting her get away with it.* Well, if that is what you want then I need my keys back." I spat.

"I'll bring your keys back. Give me some time, though. I don't want to cry in front of you. This hurts me too, you know."

I disconnected from the call and flung my phone across the room, watching the back casing and battery pop out and skitter across the floor. I didn't know how to feel, so I felt nothing. Nothing but shock and disbelief.

"Brooklyn?" Damian eased my bedroom door open, drawn by the sound of the phone breaking apart.

I stared at him, searching for some emotion, anything. Any feelings to anchor me to this moment, but I found nothing. Disbelief couldn't even cover how I felt. I was numb… perhaps it was denial. *Did that really just happen?* My head felt like it was in the clouds. It was an unpleasant, floating sensation, not unlike being in a dream. No, it had to be a nightmare. Maybe if I focused hard enough, I'd wake up soon and life could return to the way it was before.

"Are you okay?"

Wordlessly, I shook my head, the tears finally coming as my best friend wrapped his strong arms around me.

Chapter Six

CHAPTER SEVEN

This was my new reality; a life without Jesse. I wasn't adjusting well, at all. You would think that being apart from him for the month before would make this easier, but it didn't. I hadn't changed my sheets the entire time he was in the hospital, because, if I did, it would erase the memory of him. The scent of his cologne was long gone, but I still felt like his presence was there with me at night. In the silent darkness, I could still feel his heart pounding against mine as I lay on his chest after sex. He'd run his fingers along my back, causing goosebumps to form.

Deep down, I knew that if I cut off all communication with him, I would be able to move on, but I couldn't bring myself to do it. No matter how much I wanted to, I couldn't manage to stop texting or emailing every day.

I'm pathetic. It had been so good. We were like two halves of a whole. We were soul mates, and yet he easily dismissed that.

Why? I kept coming back to that question. Why wasn't I enough? Why would he have room in his heart for her, when he'd filled all of *mine*? Maybe if I knew the answer to *that*, I could let him go.

My phone pinged, which indicated an incoming text. I half-heartedly looked at the screen and my heart came alive. It was from Jesse.

Jesse:
I am going to be in the area. Can I stop by to drop off the keys?

Brooklyn:
Sure.

Jesse:
K. Leaving now.

Brooklyn:
Buckle up this time.

I'd tried to keep things light, but his silence made me second guess my little joke. Was it insensitive? Were we not able to even joke with each other anymore? I groaned out loud, pacing around my condo. Once he handed me the keys, that would be it. That would be the last nail in the coffin. There was still hope, however slight, to convince him to stay. When he saw me, he would remember our time together, the chemistry we shared.

I already knew he was prone to memories influencing him. Just look at the situation we found ourselves in.

There was no time for a shower, but I applied some makeup to make me look less like a zombie.

Jesse stepped through my patio door, his usual smile nowhere to be seen. I cupped his face, stroking his jawline and letting his longer-than-normal stubble scrape against the palms of my hands. His reaction was not what I had anticipated. Instead, he was cold, flinching at my touch. There was no love in his reaction. I tried to swallow back the tears, but there was no stopping them. He pulled me against his chest as sobs wracked my body, but he felt like a stranger. No words were spoken by either of us as he continued to do what could only be described as "his duty." He showed no remorse for the decision that had been made; no regret could be seen in his eyes. That, I think, hurt the most. Had our time together meant nothing to him? Had I seen us as something more than what we really were?

I wrapped my arms around myself, rubbing my hands up and down the length of my arms. I wasn't sure if I would ever feel warmth again. It felt as though ice ran through my veins rather than blood. I looked at the man I no longer recognized. His light was gone; the tenderness that had softened his face, the love that had made his eyes glow. Everything I had known… it was gone and there was only a shell of the man I had fallen for.

For a single moment, I observed the profile of Jesse's face and had a flashback to seventh grade. *This* was how I remembered him. My hand touched my heart as the memory struck me. You ask me to describe anyone else from his eighth grade class and I wouldn't be able to. He must have turned my head to bring such a vivid memory. None of that mattered anymore because this was the end. I had hoped that if he saw me he would change his mind, but it wasn't difficult to see that it was all for nothing.

"I would still like to see you." His words confused me. He wanted me, but he didn't. My blue eyes met his and I almost said yes. I loved his eyes; they were unique. There were times that they appeared green and other times hazel. This time, the way the light hit them, they were a beautiful shade of blue. I shook my head to clear my mind. I couldn't let anything cloud my judgement right now, even though I badly wanted to give him anything he asked for. He wanted to see me… but the love was gone from his eyes. Jesse reached for my hand and then it hit me… he wanted sex.

Sex between us had always been phenomenal, so would it be wrong? I couldn't imagine being with anyone else…

No. It would mean being close to him physically, but this time it would lack something. It would lack the connection that made it so amazing in the first place.

Jesse looked at me appraisingly and hesitated. "I am afraid you will end up hurt."

I played with the drawstring of my baggy pajama pants and I tried to play referee for the inward battle my head and heart were having. I knew what I should do, but it was drastically different than what I *wanted* to do. I rolled and unrolled the string, trying to draw out his visit. I didn't want him to leave… *ever.*

I swallowed back the lump in my throat and mustered up all the strength I could find. "And what about Melinda?"

"What about her?"

"Don't play coy. Not with me. You said you had feelings for her."

Jesse swallowed hard. "I said I had feelings. Being around her stirred up some confusing emotions. I'm not with her. I'm not going to go back to her. It's just like I told you, Babe, it wouldn't be fair to be with you while I'm thinking of her."

I choked back a sob at the endearment, clenching my hands into fists. "I think you are right. I will get hurt. You hurt me that day and you're *still* hurting me. Not only that, I think you seeing me will hinder you, rather than help. You need to focus on the task at hand, which is to figure out what is going on in your head. I also need to find myself again; to learn to love myself. It's for fate to decide if our paths will cross again."

"I shouldn't have suggested it, I'm sorry. It's, well... sex is so amazing with you." He gave me an apologetic smile.

"Yes. It really *was.*"

Just one last kiss. I looked at his full lips in longing. When he walked out those doors, it could be for the last time.

"You can kiss me." He smirked and, for a brief moment, there was a light back in his eyes.

This was a very bad idea, but I was only capable of making one mature decision a day and his lips were calling me. Maybe I wanted our last time together to never end and that's why I straddled him on the couch. It was wrong to tempt him with sex, but that was the only weapon I had left. Deep inside, I knew that it wouldn't matter; that he would still leave. I also knew that if he *did* stay, I would always wonder if it was genuine.

Our hands caressed and stroked while our bodies grinded and writhed with lust. Our kisses were fervent with need; lips clashing and tongues stroking. I nibbled on his ear lobe, my quickened breaths spurring him on. But it felt… off. This wasn't *us.* There was no *us* anymore and I needed to remember that. I still loved him with all my heart and soul, but he had built a wall around his heart so thick that I would never be able to penetrate it.

I held his face in my hands and took in every detail. He hadn't shaved in a few days and his eyes looked so tired. The soft lines on his face were gone and now they'd become deep, bringing a hardness to his features. It reminded me of a face that had been carved in stone. I wanted to caress and smooth out the lines and bring him back, but now it was time to say goodbye. There were no more tears. Those would come later, when I could no longer be in denial. Most likely in the shower, which is where I think, and have cried the most. I can't lie to myself in the shower.

"I still love you." I searched his eyes for a spark, something to tell me there was a flicker of hope, but that candle had burned out.

"I'll talk to you soon." Those were words that were said to make this moment less awkward. Just like in my dream, he didn't respond to my declaration of love. I never would have guessed that it would become a premonition.

He walked down the path toward the parking lot, out of my life, and… with my keys. The effort of running after him wasn't worth it; I'd just have to get my locks changed.

Chapter Seven

CHAPTER EIGHT

I don't know how long I stayed on my couch. Each sunrise brought a new feeling of dread. Another day I would have to face the reality of my life. *He doesn t love me. Maybe he never did.*

It felt like every day I was going through each phase of a breakup on repeat. Denial, Sadness, Anger, Hate, Regret, and right back to denial.

I'd barely eaten. Whenever I forced myself to get up from the couch, I'd grab a few crackers and cubes of cheese to munch on. The television was always on, but I just stared at it. I think I have watched this particular episode of *Supernatural* three times now. *Was it Dean, Sam, or Castiel who died?* The Winchester boys used to excite me, but not lately.

This is temporary. He will realize that he made a mistake… oh, look, Denial is back. I started to picture each emotion like that Disney movie, assigning bright colors to each one. I think Denial should be green, or maybe gray. Green was Disgust. Was Denial even in the movie? It could be green, too. After all, I was pretty disgusted by my denial and this entire situation.

I just can't imagine a future without Jesse. He's my soul mate… now, Sadness. Blue, definitely blue.

He'd always said he was fond of acting, did he lie to me this whole time? How could he do this to me… Anger, my favorite. Bright red and flaming. I grabbed fistfuls of my hair and shook my head back and forth. The crazy train would be making a stop at my front door soon, I just knew it. My only comfort was that he was suffering, too.

The lack of nutrition had finally caught up with me. I felt weak and dizzy. My mouth felt like sandpaper, and I needed a drink. There were no more bottles of water in the fridge, so I started to make my way down the stairs to grab some from the storage room. Halfway down, a wave of dizziness washed over me and I missed the next step. My hand desperately sought the handrail but failed and I toppled my way to the floor below. I only had a moment to comprehend what had happened before the pain became too much to bear and the room faded to black.

I could barely keep my head above water. No matter how much I tried to kick my legs, I couldn t seem to get them to move. My entire body felt sluggish, and everything happened in slow motion.

"Brooklyn?" My name sounded muffled under the water.

I slowly reached up to the hand being offered to me. Damian was here to help me. He would save me; he always did.

"Brooklyn?" Damian's voice was clearer now and closer.

It took a minute for my eyes to adjust, but there he was, looking down at me. His gray eyes were big with concern.

"Hi." My voice sounded hoarse and my throat felt like I had swallowed sand.

"Brooklyn," Damian breathed. "Thank God. How are you feeling?"

"Okay, I guess… but why am I here?" I struggled to work my way through the fogginess that still surrounded me. The monitors, IV bag, and the sterile look of the room made it obvious that I was in the hospital, but as to why I was here… I had no idea. I winced as my leg throbbed, and I struggled to figure out why.

"You don't remember?"

"Duh, obviously." I made a weak attempt at a smile.

"You fell down the stairs. Thank God I came by to check on you. You were extremely dehydrated and when was the last time you ate a proper meal? I am so *pissed* off at you right now." His arms crossed, and I knew he meant business.

"Aww, you still love me." My lower lip stuck out into a feigned pout.

"I am unsure of that, at this time. Jury's still out."

Womanly weapons had never worked on Damian. He probably *was* pissed off with me, but I knew it came from a good place. Some of that anger may have even been directed at himself for not noticing me struggle sooner. Or from fear that he didn't know what was happening to me. *Shit.* I needed to get him out of here somehow before he found out everything.

"I've been so tired." Almost to demonstrate my point, I rubbed my eyes and yawned. "I think I'm going to get some sleep. You don't have to stay if you don't want to."

Damian sighed, and his shoulders dropped. "I'm not leaving your side. I've been so worried about you. Let's talk about you being tired. Is this about Jesse? If he can't see how amazing you are, then he's not worth being upset over. One day, you'll find someone who will appreciate and treasure you."

Things with Jesse had been like a fairy tale; a dream come true. He had told me himself how perfect it was, and how wonderful and beautiful *I* was, yet, in the end, he didn't want me.

"This was never about me waiting for him to come back, or me wanting him to come back, it was more about how he was so willing to let go of someone who was supposedly fated to be with him, someone he felt a connection with. True love is difficult to find. Why would he give that up?" My lip quivered, and I could feel the burning in my throat. *I can t cry again. I just can t.*

"Because either you didn't mean enough to him… or you were his rebound relationship and I hate to say it, but, if that's the case… he won't be back. I'm sorry."

Damian never sugar coated anything. Sometimes I wished he did, but I knew I could count on him to be honest with me all the time. He wanted me to be realistic, and telling me what I *wanted* to hear was only going to make moving on a longer process than necessary. This was why Damian was my best friend. No, more than my best friend, he was like my brother. I knew whatever came out of his mouth was nothing but the truth.

"He broke my heart. I feel empty inside. Numb. I *know* I am a good person. I love with all of me. Why doesn't anyone ever want me?" That question had been one that I'd asked myself over and over. Sometimes, I'd wondered how I possibly even still believed in love.

"There *is* someone out there for you. You just haven't found him yet." Damian wiped a tear off my cheek with his thumb.

"We'll see." I mumbled.

"On that negative note, I'm gonna text my wife that you're okay, and ask her to bring me coffee."

"I would love one, thanks." The thought of coffee gliding down my throat was glorious.

"Nope. You get water." His serious expression was back.

"What? Why?" My petulance was unbecoming, but I wanted coffee in the worst way.

"Because… dehydrated."

"Ugh, you suck. Coffee has water in it!" Now I was the one with my arms crossed.

"Be a good girl and I'll have her bring you back a Gatorade."

"Blech. I'll just have the water." Gatorade was vile. He knew I hated it.

Although I was grateful to have Damian in my life, at that moment I wanted to be alone. I *needed* him to leave. It was exhausting trying to keep myself together, and him being here right now was somewhat like trying to stop a freight train with my bare hands. Panic clawed at my chest. I could already feel it tightening. I knew I had to try to calm down and slow down my breathing. My leg hurt, but other than that, I felt okay. At the very least, I didn't have any cramping. That had to be a good sign, right? Damian misunderstood the reason for my panic attack and grabbed my hand. His warmth, always a comfort, terrified me right now. I couldn't be here. This couldn't turn out well.

As though I had sent out a distress signal, a doctor walked in. His badge read Dr. Saunders. My hands curled into fists as I waited to hear the news. Damian gave me a quick squeeze and mouthed the word, "*ow.*" A quick scan of the doctor's face didn't reveal much in the way of which direction this conversation was going to go. He pulled up a chair and sat down, his left foot resting on the top of his right knee.

"How are you feeling, Brooklyn?" A smile revealed a perfect set of white teeth.

"Fine, I guess." I felt anything but *fine.* I knew I should go ahead and ask him what I wanted to know, but I was afraid of the answer. Afraid for my best friend to hear the answer when he didn't even know the question. My pulse sped again.

"You need to take better care of yourself." To my horror, Dr. Saunders then turned to Damian. "Since you told me otherwise when she got here, it's my pleasure to tell you that your wife is pregnant. Congratulations."

Time froze.

At least for me. The doctor had kept right on talking, as though he'd had no idea he'd just dropped a massive bomb. "No matter what may be happening in your lives, you must put her first. You're going to be parents in just a few short months and you need to be mentally and physically ready." His disapproving look was well deserved. I had been selfish and only thinking of my own pain. I knew I had to do better. If my neglect had caused her harm, I would never have forgiven myself.

"Not my wife..." Damian's steady voice belied the fury I knew waited to erupt. The water bottle in his free hand threatened to burst open from the intense grip he had on it.

"Oh. Oh, I'm sorry. I assumed..." The doctor looked mortified as he flipped frantically through my chart. He was right to be embarrassed. "Well, I apologize for blurting it out that way. You'd listed yourself on her admission paperwork on the significant other line, so I thought…"

"It's fine," I said. "I–I hadn't told him yet, but I don't mind that he knows." Vaguely, I was aware of the doctor backing out of the room, but my attention was held by the furious eyes of my best friend.

Shit! I'd always told Damian everything, and I broke his trust by keeping such a big secret from him.

"Damian, I'm sorry I…"

"*When* exactly did you plan to tell me?"

"I…" I thought about it. Honestly, I had no idea. I'd known for some time, but I'd wanted to tell Jesse first. Then everything had happened. My shoulders slumped in defeat. "Significant other line?"

"I was in a hurry, and it was the top one. Plus, I knew they wouldn't leave me in the dark then. *Unlike some people here.* Focus. What were you thinking, Brooklyn? And then starving yourself? Not staying hydrated? How could you be so stupid! It's like I don't even know who you are right now!" he spat. I flinched, knowing I deserved his anger. "The fucking donuts. Not drinking the wine. The

Twinkies. The exhaustion and moodiness. How did I not see?" His fingers raked through his hair. "That fucker abandoned you?"

"He doesn't know." I whispered.

Damian's voice dropped from shouting to a menacing whisper all at once. "Say that *one... more... time.*"

I cleared my voice and repeated the words.

Back to shouting. "You've kept this from him. What in God's name would make you think it was a good idea not to tell him?" With the volumes he was reaching, I was pretty sure that soon the entire hospital would know my secret. Hell, Jesse may hear it all the way from his place. *Or Melinda's,* I couldn't help but bitterly think.

"I wanted him to come back to me because he *wanted* to, not because he felt *obligated* to."

"Don't you think he has a *right* to know? Don't you think you should have let *him* decide what he wanted to do? Did you ever think about what you were going to do after the baby was born?"

"I haven't really thought about any of that. This wasn't how I thought things would work out!" I grabbed the water bottle that Damian had placed on my table and took a few swigs. I couldn't even look him in the face. He was right, of course, but I wouldn't be able to be content in my life if I felt like Jesse came back because he felt forced to.

"Obviously!" He turned away from me and ran his fingers through his hair in agitation. His head went back, and he stared at the ceiling, probably praying for the strength to not strangle me. Without turning around, he finished with, "I need to go do something. I'll be back."

"Please, don't tell him!" I begged.

He turned and glared at me with a fury in his eyes that I'd never seen from him before. "It's like I told you, Brooklyn. Somebody has to be the adult. I'd just hoped it would be one of you. Now it's even more important than before."

"Damian, I'm begging you…"

He left without another word. Damian and Jesse had never been close. I doubted he had any way to reach him… and he'd never gone completely against my wishes before, even when he'd said he would. I took a deep breath to fight off the panic and could only hope for the best.

Chapter Eight

CHAPTER NINE

During my fall down my stairs, I had broken my leg. I was a klutz on a good day, so working around a cast and crutches was going to be awesome. An obstetrician had come to my room later that day to lecture me on my lack of prenatal care. I was also made aware of the risks of x-rays and fetuses and had to sign off on a bunch of paperwork. My release day was tomorrow and admittedly I was a little nervous about being alone at home. Damian would have probably let me stay with him, but I didn't like to ask for help. I would manage, I just had to make sure that I stayed on the lower level of my condo.

My newfound confidence was squashed when Damian showed up, stone faced. My insides twisted; he was still angry with me.

"I have arranged to have someone help you around the house for a bit. She will make sure you *eat,* and not fall down the stairs. You are *not* going to tell me that you don't need help, because that would be a very bad idea right now. *Don't test me, Brooklyn.*" His lips curved into a fake and slightly scary smile.

"Ok, then." *Ugh.* I hated having people in my home.

"Good!" He was smirking now. *Grr.* He loved it when he got his way and was taking some perverse pleasure in this.

Something else I hated was hospital food, but I wasn't about to ask Damian to get me take out. He would most likely tell me that hospital food was good for me and I didn't deserve take out.

In some ways I was grateful to be going home, but in another way, I wasn't looking forward to it at all. I had to remind myself that whomever this was would only be there for a few weeks. If I could prove that I could take care of myself then maybe she would leave even sooner.

Damian brought me home after I was discharged. He had been to my condo at some point and Brooklyn-proofed everything. I was set up in the spare room downstairs and he even went as far as to put child gates at the stairs. *Seriously?* When I questioned him about it, he said that since I'd acted like a child, I'd be treated like a child. Besides, I was a klutz and he had to make sure that all bases were covered. I refrained from pointing out that, unlike a child, I had the fine motor skills to remove the gates at any time.

He tucked me into bed and said that the nurse would be arriving soon, and he would check on me later. It was nice to be back in my bed with the feather pillows and the fluffy duvet. I supposed it might be nice to be pampered for a while.

I awoke to the sound of dishes being moved about in the kitchen. The nurse must be here. *Ugh.* I was by no means a people person. I liked my space and would consider myself a shy person. I could wait in the bedroom and pretend I was sleeping or I could get this over with now. She's going to be here for the next few weeks and I was going to have to accept that. It wasn't worth pushing things with Damian by sending her away.

I lifted my heavily casted leg over the edge of the bed. The crutches had been strategically placed so they were within reach. I haven't had the chance to practice much on them, so it was going to be interesting. Maybe it was good that Damian blocked the stairways, not that I'd ever admit that to him.

I grunted my way out of the bedroom and into the kitchen. The first thing I noticed was the red hair. *It couldn t be.* Melinda turned around and didn't appear shocked that she was in my home. Her eyes zeroed in on my belly and she sneered in disgust. I felt like a prey animal that was about to be eaten by her predator. My bedroom door was behind me and if I was quick enough, I could lock myself in there, but there was no point in even trying with a broken leg and crutches to deal with.

"Here, let me help you. You should sit and relax." She practically skipped over to me with an enthusiasm that made me leery. My crutches were removed from under my arms and leaned against the wall beside Melinda. There was no way I could reach them. Melinda had me lean against her and with her support, I was placed onto the sofa in the living room.

"So…" she clapped her hands together. "What would you like to eat?" In my mind, I imagined her rubbing her hands together as she thought of ways to slip poison into my food.

"I'm not really hungry, but thanks anyway." I returned her fake smile with one of my own. I was anything but happy. Deep inside, I was terrified of this woman being in my home. The entire time I'd been with Jesse, she'd conspired against us, against *me*… and now I was essentially trapped with her in my own home. My phone was in my bedroom, so I had no way of contacting anyone. Maybe Damian would show up like he said he would and save the day. This would be an excellent time for him to turn up with his famously good timing.

Melinda tsked at me, shaking her head. "Now, now. I am here to make sure that you are being taken care of, and I wouldn't be doing my job if I didn't make sure you eat."

"Maybe later."

She was now behind the counter and rifling through the cupboard below. When she stood up she had a revolver in her hand, pointed directly at me.

"Okay, okay, I'll eat." It was the first thing I could think of to say.

"You don't listen very well, do you?" she snarled.

"I… I'm not sure what you mean?" This was it. This may very well be my last day. Instinctively, I placed the throw pillow in front of my stomach. It was ridiculous to think that a bullet would not pierce through the fabric, but it was the only thing I could reach to protect my baby.

"You should have stayed away from what's mine."

"You and Jesse have been separated for three years and you are the one who left him. What makes you think he's yours?" It was probably not advisable to be arguing with a gun-wielding, mad woman, but my temper got the best of me. *Damn temper.*

"He still loves me. Isn't that why he left you? I told you that day in the hospital that we'd be a family again. You didn't believe me. You told me to do my worst. Challenge accepted, *bitch.*"

Melinda's cat-like eyes stared at my stomach. I could almost sense her drawing a target over the pillow I clutched fiercely to my stomach before she continued. "He will be back in my arms soon enough but with a baby on the way… that could cause problems."

"Jesse doesn't even know about the baby. He doesn't need to know. If you let me go, I will move far away from here, so he never has to see me." The words rushed out of my mouth before I had a chance to even think if that scenario was possible. I would say and do anything to protect my child, even if it meant never seeing Jesse again.

"I made sure you weren't allowed to visit Jesse in the hospital, but, even after that, you insisted on texting him. He never got them, by the way. I made sure to delete them all. I thought you were a smart girl and would take the hint that you didn't belong in our family." Melinda was waving the gun around in the air as she spoke, like it was a prop in a movie and not a deadly weapon.

"I'm so sorry, Melinda. I didn't mean to hurt your family. It was selfish of me." Lying had never been my thing, but desperate times called for desperate measures. Despite everything that had happened, I would never regret my time with Jesse.

"Yes, it was!" With each word she pointed the gun in my direction. She was crying and the way her mascara smeared her eyes, it only made her look even more deranged.

"Melinda, you need to put the gun down." Jesse spoke authoritatively, his unexpected voice without any trace of fear.

I desperately wanted to be thankful that Jesse was here, but now he was in danger. My hope was that Melinda's love for Jesse would protect him. She seemed lost without him.

"Jesse? What are you doing here?" In her moment of distraction, the gun was shifted away from my general direction.

As Jesse spoke, he slowly moved toward the couch I sat on. "Looking for you, of course. I can't stay away from you any longer. The home health service gave me this address."

"Why would they do that? And how did you get in here? I thought I locked the doors." She sounded doubtful. I guess the idea that he had my key never occurred to her.

"The back door was unlocked. You must have forgotten that one." It was a lie and I knew it, because that one was always locked. Fate had been at work again. Jesse forgetting to give me my keys back and me never changing the locks… it was meant to happen this way.

"Come on, Melinda. Put the gun away for me? There is no reason to hurt Brooklyn. I choose you. We can't be together if you kill her and end up in prison." Jesse's hands raised slowly as he continued to walk past the couch toward Melinda.

"What about the baby?" she spat out.

"Brooklyn will live her life and we will live ours. I don't want anything to do with *it*," he said with disgust.

He knows about the baby. He wasn't here for Melinda. He was here for me. Damian had to have gotten to him. At that moment, I wasn't sure whether to be livid that he put Jesse in danger by telling him, or if I was grateful that he came here and could possibly save us all from harm.

I couldn't see Jesse's face, only his back, but his muscles were tight with tension. Deep down, I knew that he was only saying those things to appease Melinda, but I still couldn't help feeling the cold tendrils of jealousy creep through my soul. He had very much loved her at one time, and maybe he still did in a way, but over time people can change and they aren't the same person you fell in love with. Right now, I couldn't understand what he ever saw in her.

"We need to get rid of that baby. If we don't it will always be a presence in our lives, whether we actually see it or not!" Her hands shook as she aimed the gun directly at me. Her finger was on the trigger and with all her shaking, I was afraid she would accidentally pull it.

Jesse must have sensed it too, because he leapt in front of me. The sudden movement caused her to jump in surprise and she pulled the trigger twice.

Everything happened in a blur. All the sounds were amplified; the click of the trigger being pulled, the *bang* of the gun going off, Melinda's screams. Jesse fell to the floor as if in slow motion, blood pooling everywhere and staining the carpet around him. I felt my heart breaking as I crawled to him, dragging my leg behind me in a whirlwind of pain. It felt like I was in quicksand, the mud making my progress sluggish.

"Jesse..." I breathed. "Stay with me."

Blood bubbled from his mouth as he struggled for each and every rattling breath. The wound looked horrible. She'd missed his heart, striking just to the left of it. For a moment I hoped that was a good sign, but watching him labor to breathe, hearing his pain-filled gasps, told me his lung was punctured and he was literally drowning in horrid agony in front of me.

My chest hurt. My heart was broken. All I could do was hope against hope that somehow someone would find us in time. I felt something hard pressing against my thigh and looked down to find Jesse's cell phone, 911 displayed brightly on the screen and the seconds counting up.

Jesse had come for me.

I pressed my hand to my chest and brushed my lips across his forehead. "Please don't die," I begged.

His hand lifted gently to my neck. "Brookl... I... love... sorry."

I laid in his arms as he took his last painful breaths. Blood seeped out like a bubbling brook from his chest and mouth, staining his Metallica shirt. The sound of the gun firing replayed over and over in my mind until I wasn't sure how many times she'd really fired it. *This is a dream. This can't be happening.* A bullet sat lodged near his heart, the heart that belonged to me. I rubbed my chest to relieve the discomfort. It felt almost as if I had been shot as well, but the blood that covered me was his.

"I love you. I'm sorry," had been his last words to me. I didn't even have the chance to say the same before he'd shuddered and the light in his beautiful hazel eyes dimmed forever.

The paramedics arrived, and there was still a glimmer of hope that he would come back to me, but our connection was severed; ripped away. The bond between two soul mates was a rare thing, and now it was gone forever.

CHAPTER TEN

Emptiness. That is all there was. My future, my hope, my soul mate, my child… they had all been taken away from me. I felt lost in my own apartment. I no longer belonged here, yet, something held me, forcing me to remain. Maybe it was Damian. I hadn't spoken to him since Jesse died. I knew he would have done everything he could to help me work through this pain, but for some reason I didn't *want* to feel better.

I picked up my phone and dialed Damian's number. It rang twice before he picked up. There was a pause before he spoke.

"H-Hello?" His voice wavered, and I knew I wasn't ready to talk. Instead of saying anything, I hung up. It was easier that way. If I'd spoken he would have made me stay on the phone.

It had been days since I'd left the condo. Perhaps staying in the place where Jesse and our baby had their lives ripped from them was making things worse. I had not attended Jesse's funeral. I couldn't bring myself to watch him being lowered into the ground forever. It would have made his death even more real. It was time that I take the first step to my healing. It was time I went to visit his grave.

My fingertips ran over the engraved letters on the tomb stone. *Jesse Carson.* I leaned against the stone and rested my head. It was a cold, winter day, much colder than the day Jesse took me out to the lake. I wrapped my arms around myself, though I didn't feel anything. The tombstone beside Jesse had fresh flowers, too. I examined that name as well, and froze. I couldn't move. This couldn't be right… *Brooklyn Johnson.*

"Babe, it's time."

"Jesse?"

He had his hand extended for me to take it. I didn't ask where we were going. It didn't matter, as long as it was with him. We were reunited once again, and my heart felt like it could finally beat again.

"I am your heart. I am your light. Let my love heal you." Those were the words I had spoken to him, back when he was in the hospital. "Let's go home."

We walked down the cobblestone path hand in hand, the light surrounding us with its warmth.

Fate always wins.

Chapter Ten

EPILOGUE

The End_

The X-screen cursor once again blinked in sync with my heart, a hypnotic rhythm. An unseasonable cold draft blew right through me, making my teeth chatter. The window was closed, but it was an old house, so maybe it wasn't sealed very well.

I stretched my arms into the air as though in victory and stifled a yawn. It was late, and my bed was calling me.

I waved my hand and made the gesture needed to send the manuscript to my printer. A second wave made the virtual screen disappear into darkness. Tomorrow I would read through it and revise it before handing it off to my agent.

The comforting sound of the paper feeding into my printer filled my ears as I made my way to my room. Finishing a book was the most euphoric feeling in the world and this story, particularly, felt different. It was difficult to explain. It had almost been as though the story had flowed through my fingertips. No thinking required. I felt so accomplished, so… happy, I'd all but forgotten my problems with Lukas. He wasn't worth my tears, anyway.

I fell into a peaceful and easy sleep, a smile playing on my lips.

The stack of paper felt heavy in my hand. I thumbed through the manuscript, and watched the letters as they almost seemed to move across the page like a movie. A page came loose from the pile and fluttered to the floor. I reached down to pick it up but instead of grabbing the page, my hand grabbed my chest. Have I lost it? Below the inscription "The End" there were words that hadn't been there the night before. I'd been exhausted last night but in no way intoxicated. I *definitely* would have remembered going back to the X-screen to add more to the story… wouldn't I? I scooped up the paper and folded it. It would be easier to deny this had happened if I couldn't see it. Out of sight, out of mind.

I sat down heavily in my chair to plan out my next move. It wasn't possible I was losing my mind, was it? Could someone have broken in and added to my story as a prank?

I may not have been drunk last night, but I certainly would be now. The cork in the champagne bottle made a popping sound as it was pulled. The sound of the liquid hitting the bottom of the glass and the slight fizzing of the bubbles felt comforting. Soon I'd feel all warm and fuzzy and ready to tackle this new addition to my previously completed story.

Taking a deep breath, I unfolded the paper and smoothed out the creases.

We ve been by your side, watching you grow up into a beautiful young woman. We know you are struggling, my darling. You see the world as a cruel place. You no longer believe in love and I am here to tell you not to give up… fate will never pass you by.

You were made with love. The day of his car accident, your father had been on his way to see me and I was going to tell him about you…

The night we both died was both a blessing and a curse. I got my Jesse back, I got to tell him about you, and you survived. Since the day you were born, you ve always been a fighter. Don t give up on love. If it is meant to be, fate will make it happen. We left the world in each other s arms and are together still. We love you.

Please tell Damian that he needs to forgive himself. I ve seen him battle, these many years, with feeling responsible for our deaths... None of it was his fault, and we are forever grateful to him for watching over you. This was fate... everything worked out as it was supposed to. We are together. We love you very much.

I reread the passage probably a dozen times. A lump formed in my throat, and I didn't even try to fight the tears that poured down my cheeks. I'd never known my birth parents, but now I felt a connection with them.

There was a phone call I had to make, and my heart nearly pounded out of my chest as my shaking hands dialed the number.

"Hey, Jessilyn. You're up early. You okay?" He may be my adopted father, but he has been there for me since the day I was born, always looking out for me, always so kind and loving.

"I'm fine, Dad. Are you sitting down?"

The distinctive squeak of the kitchen chair could be heard through the phone.

"Okay, I'm sitting and bracing myself." There was a slight tension to his voice. He wasn't kidding. "You aren't pregnant, are you?"

"No!" I squealed.

"That's a relief. That asshole you're with isn't good enough for my little girl."

"Well, we've broken up and he's ancient history now. Well, as ancient as thirty-six hours can be. But that's not my news, Dad." The annoyance bled into my voice.

"Okay, okay. Tell me your news. I'm listening."

"Mom left me a message."

"Um, okay. She just left for work… I don't understand why I needed to sit for that."

"My birth mom… Brooklyn. She wanted me to tell you that what happened was not your fault and you have to stop blaming yourself." The words escaped my lips in a rush. Maybe I was afraid I would lose my nerve. I had to admit, this whole thing was like something from the twilight zone.

"Jessilyn… that's… that's impossible. She couldn't have written anything to either of us."

"She did, Dad. Last night. She came to me and wanted me to tell you that."

His stuttered inhalation was my only answer.

"Dad?"

"I can't do this over the phone. I'm on my way over."

Click.

Well, he didn't sound like he didn't believe me, so I supposed that was a good sign.

"Where is this message?" My dad flung open my front door, his hair disheveled and I imagined him running his hands through his hair on the drive over. He always did that when he was upset.

"Come on in… and hello to you, too."

I set a coffee mug down at my kitchen table.

"I may need something stronger than that, if what you're claiming is true. How are you so calm about this?" His gray eyes had taken on a crazed look.

I added a generous splash of Bailey's to each mug.

"I wasn't at first. You know the story I've been writing?"

"No."

"Well, I suppose that's because I wrote pretty much all of it yesterday. Anyway, the point is… I think Mom was writing it *through* me."

I slid the manuscript across the table toward my dad with the note on top. I watched his eyes move back and forth across the white page. When he looked up he was crying. I'd never seen my dad cry before. I got up from my chair and we held each other as he sobbed into my shoulder.

"The nurse who came to take care of your mother was Melinda, Jesse's ex-wife. I'd had no idea. If I hadn't arranged for her to be there… If I'd hadn't been…" He paused to regain control of himself. "When she was given your mother's file she knew about the pregnancy and went into a jealous rage. She brought a gun with her and was going to kill your mother, but Jesse jumped in the way. He was there because I went against your mother's wishes and told him about you. I'd never once betrayed her like that before. She was my best friend, closer than a sister. My betrayal that day caused two deaths. The nurse your mother didn't even want wound up killing her. It was all my fault. I practically pulled the trigger myself. I am so sorry, Jessilyn. You didn't get to know your parents because of me. They managed to perform an emergency C-Section on your mother and even though the odds were stacked against you, you survived. She was only twenty-four weeks along on the day she died. You were born sixteen weeks early and, somehow, miraculously weren't hurt when your mother was shot in the chest. You were so tiny, but you were determined, and stubborn. Just like your mother. You remind me so much of her. Anyway… eventually, I could hold you and as soon as I had you in my arms, I knew I could never let you go. A few days after she died, I received a phone call from your mother's cell phone, but when I answered there was no one there. I wanted to believe it was her trying to communicate with me." He gave a shaky chuckle. "Probably to scold me that she'd begged me not to tell him. I deserved her wrath. I *don't* deserve her forgiveness."

My heart ached for my dad. He was so torn up and had lived with the guilt for so long.

"Dad, Mom sent that message because she wants you to stop suffering. She and dad are together. They are at peace and now it is time for you to do the same. That's what she wants… and it's what I want, too."

"Here's my manuscript, Susie." I set the package on her desk enthusiastically.

"Well, from the excerpts you've sent me, I think it may be a winner." She paused and then tapped the package sitting at the corner of her desk. "You know… from what you described, this isn't your usual style of writing. It should prove to be refreshing. What brought on the change?"

"You never know. Maybe I was possessed by a ghost." I winked.

AFTERWORD
BY DAVID S. SCOTT

Never piss off an author. They'll just make your literary death as painful as possible.

That could be the moral of this piece. Anyway, we hope you enjoyed *Fading Light*. Parts of it were difficult to write. It's not always easy bleeding one's thoughts and ideas onto paper. Life, death, love, and guilt… lessons we all learn as we all walk our various paths. We tried to capture everything in this romantic suspense novella. Some parts were based on true events, and some parts were not, except in our imaginations.

If you enjoyed it, I hope you'll be compelled to leave a review and tell your friends. If you didn't enjoy it, we still gladly welcome your reviews and thoughts. Just be sure to read the first line of this afterword, first. ;)

Chapter One of David S. Scott's
Upcoming Release

OBSIDIAN ANGEL

This book is a work in progress, any or all of the following may change between now and it's release.

We were the stuff of legends.

Angels, some called us. Others, demons. *Vampyr* …

What we were was all of the above, or maybe none at all.

We were the *Nefthiri*. The closest translation in the human tongue would be "hunters" or "rangers." Our calling was to be the guardians and gatekeepers of both our world of Dunia and the human Earth.

I stood stock still, a silent sentinel atop the towering office building. The night was dark, and I knew none of the near-sighted humans scurrying below could see me, even had they the foresight to look up. Even so, I wasn't taking any chances. I'd cloaked myself in solid black clothing and released my shoulder length black hair to hang freely around my pale face, casting it in shadow.

Cocking my head, I scanned the ground below for my prey, a rogue doppelganger. I'd been tracking him for weeks, following the trail of human bodies. Nasty race, doppelgangers. They were shapeshifters, able to take the form of anyone they chose. Intelligent, cruel. They would stalk their prey, memorize patterns in their day-to-day routine, take on the form of someone they trusted, then they would strike.

Doppelgangers prized intelligence above all else. Was it any wonder that the only thing they would target in their victim was their brain?

Luckily, there weren't many of them and they didn't need to feed often. The smarter ones knew to only go after the dredges of society, those who wouldn't be missed.

I had no idea why this particular one was on a killing spree.

A scream pierced the night. My amber eyes locked on the source: a young couple just below me in a secluded alley. Even from this height, I could see the telltale signs of the male's otherworldly aura, like a personal signature.

Taking a deep breath, I stepped over the ledge.

I reveled in the liberation of my freefall as the ground rose to meet me. Four hundred yards left to go … three hundred yards, then two. I released my obsidian wings, exulting in the strength of them as they unfolded and slowed my descent.

Thump. I landed hard, the momentum of my dive forcing me to kneel. Crouching down, I glared at the pair in front of me, my wings still spread wide and draped across the ground like a long, silky curtain.

"Ash."

The menacing tone mocked me, grating on my nerves. I rose to my feet, fingering the wickedly curved blade at my belt. "My reputation proceeds me, I see. Who are you, asshole?"

A wheezing laugh was my answer. "Ah ah ah … you know that names have power."

My left wing shot forward and slammed the doppelganger in the head, bowling him over. The human female who accompanied him, formerly silent, screamed and ran away, her heels clicking loudly on the cement. I let her go, she wasn't my concern.

I regarded the doppelganger as he rose to his feet. "You're a threat to all of us with your actions."

"Come now, Ash, they're just humans." He swiped at his bleeding nose with the back of his hand. "Their lives last but a minute, anyway. What different does it make?"

"You know our laws. I've come to deport you back to Dunia."

The doppelganger flickered as his appearance began to change. His short brown hair lengthened, darkened, until they were an inky black and hung in sheets around his face. His gray irises expanded and mutated to a bright amber shade. His nose became more angular, and his jawline more severe. His clothes even darkened to match mine and he grew in height until we were identical in every way, aside from my wings, which he was unable to mimic.

"Tell me, *Nefthiri*, do you like who you see when you look in the mirror?"

We lunged at the same time, both drawing identical swords. On instinct, I raised the wicked-looking serrated sweeping blade to parry the incoming assault. Sparks flew and twin blades rang out. Puzzling. This brand of trickster should not be able to mimic magical items like this. I retracted my wings, I'd handle this one from the ground.

I deflected a few more blows, feeling him out with every strike. His swings were wild, untrained. He expelled unnecessary effort with each one and would tire soon at this rate. I just needed to wait for my opening.

My sword was a key. Lightning danced along its blade, and with the proper application, could open a gateway between this world and the next. I could choose to deport this wretch, or I could destroy him. His mimicry of my weapon, however, concerned me. Was it functional?

It certainly looked it.

If I killed him, I'd never learn how he learned to do that. Damn him.

"Shall I take that as a no?" he asked.

"Fuck off, dirtbag. No more tricks."

"*Tricksss?*" he hissed as our swords crashed together once more. "I don't know what you're talking about."

"You know, that's a nice weapon you have there. Tell me about it."

"This old thing? I took it from the body of the last *Nefthiri* I came across. Handy, I'll give it that."

I faltered. "What?"

"Ah, I think you knew him. Stone."

I blocked another strike and pushed back. I was done with this bullshit. Time to get serious. Forget deporting him. He'd killed one of my brothers, and avenging his death was both my duty and a pleasure. I spun around on the balls of my feet and ducked, slashing out as his weapon whistled over my head. My aim was true and I connected with his abdomen.

The doppelganger screamed. Blood flowed from the injury, covering my hand. Curling my lip in distaste, I twisted the blade, still buried in his gut. My amber eyes met his identical ones as I yanked the weapon from his gut and shoved him to the ground. Fear contorted his face, or was it mine? No matter. His mind games wouldn't sway me.

I raised the sword and plunged it into the trickster's heart, ending the man who looked like me. After a beat, the doppelganger shifted, his features blurring in my vision. I watched as he reverted back to his natural form, then grabbed him and brought his neck to my lips. My fangs extended, razor sharp. Unable to wait any longer, I pressed them into his jugular vein and drained him. His pulse was already slowing, but it didn't matter. Despite the horrible way Doppelganger blood tasted, it was still potent. With every swallow, I felt reinvigorated, felt his energy becoming mine.

I drank my fill, until the being in my arms was nothing but a dried out husk. Doppelganger's true forms were hideous to behold. Greenish-gray mottled skin, large eyes, completely bald. Humans who saw them called them aliens. There was a place out in New Mexico where they had found a few of them. Area 51, I think they called it.

What to do with the body?

I rose to my feet and regarded it, curling my lip in distaste. I wiped down my sword and shoved it back into its scabbard, then picked up Stone's weapon and sheathed it, as well.

My options were few. I could destroy or stash the body here, or I could bring it back to Dunia. The only problem with that was—

The sound of a woman's voice from around the nearby corner caught my attention. Her terrified whisper told me she was afraid and didn't want to be overheard.

"Stupid phone. Work! Emergency calls shouldn't need reception."

More alarming was the tinny voice I heard suddenly answer her.

"911, what is your emergency?"

"I'm not sure. My boyfriend was just murdered in front of me."

"Are you somewhere safe?"

I closed the distance to the woman with supernatural speed.

"Yes. I'm close by, but he can't hear me from here. He didn't chase me when I ran."

"Where are you?"

"Hudson Street and Fifth. In an alley. I–"

I swatted the phone from her hand and stomped on it, disconnecting the call. God damn her. Human cops would be all over this area in a matter of moments.

The girl opened her mouth and screamed.

I narrowed my eyes, then grabbed her and threw her over my shoulder. Quickly, I rushed back to the doppelganger's body and scooped him up, too. In the distance, I could hear sirens approaching. I only had minutes left. I released my wings and took off into the sky, carrying both my passengers and heading to the top of the tallest building. I couldn't go far bearing their combined weights.

The girl struggled and squirmed, still screaming like a banshee.

"You need to stop that. You wouldn't want me to drop you from this height. Be still for a minute, damn you." My voice was quiet but demanding. Despite the wind rushing through our ears and her screams, I knew she could hear me. She continued to shriek and cry, but stopped writhing.

Reaching my destination, I dropped the corpse unceremoniously on the roof, then landed with a *thump.* Carefully, I lowered the finally-silent woman down and released her, trying not to notice all of her soft curves as she slid down my body. Her light blonde hair was mussed, her crystalline blue eyes were puffy and her lips were swollen from crying.

Damn it. Drinking blood always revitalized me in *every* way, really got my own blood flowing. I hated that I was noticing this woman's body at all. I curled my upper lip in distaste. It didn't matter how soft this woman was; she was a human, she was the source of no end of trouble, and touching her was beneath me.

I glared at her as her knees gave out and she tumbled to the floor.

"What did you do that for?" I demanded, retracting my wings into my back.

"Huh?" She stared at me in consternation, dazed.

"You called the cops!"

"You killed Brandon!"

I rolled my eyes heavenward and counted to ten. Pointing to the corpse on the ground, I snarled, "Does that look like anyone named Brandon? Besides, he attacked me first!"

She looked at the body and gasped. "What did you do to him?"

"Brandon is God-only-knows-where right now, probably safe, unless that bastard killed him. He is a doppelganger. A face-stealer."

"What *are* you?"

I gave a short bark of laughter. "*Now* you think to ask me that? Never you mind what I am, sweetheart. All you need to know is that I saved your life. Come to think of it, I saved your life and then you called the cops on me!"

I ran my hands through my hair and glared at her, frustrated. I had no idea what to do now. I had this woman who had seen too much, knew too much. I couldn't let her go, not like this. Not now. I needed to get her memories wiped and I had a body to dispose of.

"You couldn't just run away to the safety of your own home and doubt what you'd seen *there*, could you? That's what all the others do, damn it!" I began to pace on the rooftop, my mind whirling. "Now what am I going to do with you?"

She paled. "What *are* you going to do with me?"

At least she had stopped screaming. That was improvement. I stopped pacing and regarded her in silence. There was only one solution. I drew my sword and held it aloft, my posture menacing.

"No, please. I'm sorry! I'm so sorry," she sobbed.

"Hold on to me."

"I–what?"

"This will be disorienting. Hold on to me."

Her forehead wrinkled, confusion clouding her eyes. With a sigh I grabbed hold of her and held her tight to my chest, then activated the weapon. The world around us appeared to spin, faster and faster. Lightning flickered in the sky, and thunder rumbled. The annoying woman trembled in my arms and I held her tighter. I held the blade high in the air. Lightning shot down and joined with it, splitting off to form a triangular door, with the sword marking the highest point. I released the weapon and it hovered in midair, maintaining the power. With one arm, I reached down and threw the corpse through the door.

"Ready?" I shouted over the wind

"No!"

Hiding my smirk, I grabbed my sword and pulled, carrying the infuriating woman through the door, which closed behind us.

Chapter One of Melissa Ann's upcoming Release

Chapter One of Melissa Ann's
Upcoming Release

MIRRORED SOULS

Analiese didn't think anything could ever compare to the physical pain of childbirth. She was wrong. When her daughter was taken away the ache in her heart was unbearable.

Each cry she heard brought her closer to the brink of hysterics. Desperation clawed at her, and frustration at knowing there was very little she could do had her shaking uncontrollably. She wanted to hold her newborn but all she could do was watch her being taken away.

"This child is damned. She bears the witches mark." Analiese's mother had stated without an ounce of sympathy for her own daughter or the granddaughter she now held in her arms. How could she be so callous. Couldn't she see that this beautiful baby was innocent? Analiese's mother

thrust the baby into the neighbour's hands. "Remove the demon spawn from my presence, Catherine."

"Mama! No!" Analiese sobbed, the pain from childbirth forgotten in her need to fight for the life of her child. She knew death was the punishment for bearing the witches mark. This child would not see another day.

Analiese pulled aside the blankets and hoisted herself up to sit on the edge of the bed. Still weak from the long and difficult labor, Analiese fought against the dizziness. With shaky legs she started to shuffle towards Catherine, her right hand reaching toward her friend and neighbor and the other holding her belly.

"Please! Please don't take her from me." Analiese's voice trembled, thick with emotion. Tears streamed down from bloodshot eyes.

Catherine regarded Analiese, her brow furrowed with indecision. A myriad of emotions flitted across her face: guilt, pity, and perhaps even fear. Catherine had been her best friend ever since

Analiese moved to Salem. She was the only one Analiese confided in about the father and the baby and now she had been appointed the duty of having the child destroyed. Her agony-filled eyes darted from the helpless baby to Analiese. Tears streamed down her face and, for a moment, it looked like Catherine was going to bring the baby to Analiese. Catherine's jaw set, resolved. She spun on her heel and raced through the door

Analiese tried to run after her. She would leave the village if it meant saving her baby. That was pretty much guaranteed since she was an unwed mother with a baby and no known husband. She made it through the door but collapsed on the dirt outside. Analiese cried out in agony, gripping her stomach as blood dripped in a steady stream down her leg, staining her simple white shift. The pain was a welcome distraction from the agony of her shattered heart, her spirit destroyed along with her daughter.

Analiese whispered, "Goodbye, Emma. I'm so sorry I couldn't save you. I'm sorry I never got to hold you… not even once. I'll always love you." She laid upon the cold earth and wrapped her arms around her knees, sobs wracking her body. Regret seized her heart and tightened the knot in her belly. Impotent rage flooded her body, igniting her flesh with invisible flames. She felt as though she would explode from all the emotions invading her. The only thing Analiese could do in hopes to relieve some of these feelings was to scream. Her shrieks reached the darkest corners of her village, heard by nearby townsfolk. Analiese continued to lie on the dirt-covered ground even when the rain began to pour. The very heavens seemed to share her pain with her. The blood washed from her legs and mixed with the mud beneath her body. Analiese's clothes were soaked and hugged her bare body, exposing the flesh that had been covered by the thin, white, shift. Even her mother had abandoned her, uncaring what happened to her disgrace of a daughter. Analiese no longer belonged here among her friends and fellow villagers, she was an outcast. She needed to find a new place to live, somewhere no one knew of her and her tarnished past.

Albany awoke from her violent shivering. Her wet clothes pressed against her naked skin causing goosebumps to form on her chilled flesh. Confused, she threw back the bedding, intent on jumping into the shower to warm herself back up. Albany froze, horrified and shocked by what she found under the covers, making her forget about the warmth she had so desperately wanted. Mud was caked on her pajamas and smeared among the sheets. Albany rushed to the mirror to make sure this want a figment of her imagination. She frowned. This was her room but everything was a mirror image and run down. The walls were water stained and the paint was peeled from the walls. Her pale face stared back at her, devoid of makeup. Her hair was covered by a linen hat and the garments were not from this time. A brown fitted waistcoat, petticoat and white apron covered a familiar shift. What was happening? With effort, she tore her eyes away from the mirror to get confirmation of whatever this was, but her room was as it always has been. She could still smell traces of the paint recently used to freshen up the door frame. She turned back to the mirror and continued to stare in bafflement over her new wardrobe but the image in the mirror had faded and Albany was back in her time, her room. She squeezed her eyes shut and peeked through her partially closed eyes at her image once more. Mud still marred her pajamas. What could this mean? Albany had a feeling that it was more than a simple case of sleep walking, but to think it was anything else was crazy. She took long cleansing breaths to try to calm her frantically beating heart. Panic crept its way past the denial as she watched dried mud flake off her clothes and onto the hardwood floor. She eyed the broom but decided to shower first and sweep last. Perhaps after washing the sleep from her eyes she would come back out here and everything would be as it should, no dirt on the floor or mud smeared on her sheets.

Albany hissed when the hot water hit her. It had only taken a few moments for the initial sting of the water to become soothing and thaw her half-frozen skin. Beyond the shower curtain laid the evidence of something she couldn't even begin to wrap her mind around. Albany was not a skeptic, she possessed special abilities, but nothing she'd ever done before could explain away any of this. Her skin was pink by the time she was ready to face her reality. She peeked out from behind the shower curtain and towards the pile of clothes that had been discarded. No, no, no. With her head grasped in her hands she shook her head, trying to refute what her eyes could plainly see. She quickly got dressed and proceeded to violently rip the sheets off the bed she shared with her husband, Jaydon. More tangible proof of what she did indeed experience. Thankfully, Jaydon was out of town and not here to witness her mental breakdown, or whatever this was. She stopped in front of the mirror and stared at her reflection. Albany held an armful of dirty laundry, her black hair shone in the sunlight and no linen hat covered her head.

Her gaze became distant as she recalled the day she had hung the mirror that she had found covered and hidden in a dusty room in her yet-to-be-renovated home…

Albany wiped the glass surface with window cleaner, but it was still clouded. There was a sliver of the glass missing from the corner of the mirror but Albany didn't mind, she planned to replace it with a new piece of glass anyway. She dropped the soiled paper towels into a wastepaper basket and grabbed a rag that she had made using an old shirt. Silvo was dabbed onto a rag and Albany worked the cloth over the silver frame with patience and thoroughness. The silver gleamed brightly which made the cloudiness of the glass more pronounced with the exception of the absent piece of mirror. She questioned what had happened all those years ago to cause this once perfect surface to become flawed. Albany's fingers lightly traced the broken edge and thought about what this mirror had once witnessed all those years ago, how much the image it reflected, differed. Who else had looked in this same mirror? Where had this mirror once hung? Albany was yanked from her reverie by a sharp pain lancing through her finger. She instinctively jerked her hand away and stuck the injured finger into her mouth, tasting the metallic flavor of blood.

Albany's eyes refocused and shifted to the missing piece of mirror. She had never replaced the glass like she had first planned. After all, replacing it would be stripping away part of its history. The clothes and bedding were dropped to the floor. Albany ran her fingertip along the slightly raised scar. *Even after all this time it was still visible. After cutting herself she had gone into the bathroom to clean and wrap it and when she had returned the once-foggy mirror was clear. She'd felt confused, but convinced herself that it was the fumes from the cleaner that were messing with her.*

Albany ran her hand along the metal frame. She could feel the vibration emanating from the mirror. The inexplicable tingling sensation gave her the wild fantasy that the mirror was somehow alive. She quickly pulled her hand away and shook her head. A mirror can't be alive, but she couldn't help but remember the day she found the mirror.

"Oh, my god, Jaydon. Look at what I found in the attic! It's a little tarnished and aged but with a little elbow grease, I bet I could make it look like new."

"You found it in the attic?" Confusion was evident on his face.

"Yes. It was leaning against the back wall."

"That's strange. I looked in that room and there was nothing in there. It was completely empty." His forehead wrinkled in confusion. "Are you sure you found it in the attic?"

"Yes, I am sure I found it in the attic. It's not my fault you're obviously blind as a bat." Albany shook her head and smirked. "You obviously overlooked it. Somehow."

Jaydon shook his head. "No way. That creepy old thing was not there before."

The old mirror glinted, looking innocent enough. Something had felt off, though. It wasn't like Jaydon to miss things, he was normally so observant. Something felt… off.

While she waited for the clothes to wash, Albany sat with her herbal tea on the front porch. Her hands surrounded the cup seeking comfort from the heat emanating from it. The air outside was cool but she couldn't shake the chill that seemed to penetrate her very bones.

Albany sighed. Was she losing her mind? How could any of this be happening?

Albany's thoughts drifted to her mother, Amaris, banished to the psych ward when she was only three. She supposed that people may find it shocking that she didn't visit her mother but truth be told, when she had visited her mother stared at her blankly, as though she was a stranger. Her mother was gone, her body merely an empty shell. If you looked into her blue eyes there was no life there, no inner light, just an opaque window to her soul. Guilt crept in and settled ever so delicately on her chest. Instinctively her hand rubbed at it trying to ease some of the pressure. Albany didn't even know if Amaris was alive, but was certain her mother was too crazy to care if she was alive. Could her insanity be hereditary?

Albany went inside and grabbed her laptop. She sat at the kitchen table and typed the name of the last known facility her mother had stayed. It suddenly became imperative that she knew what happened to Amaris, even after all these years of not seeing her.

ABOUT MELISSA ANN

Melissa Ann lives in the Great White North in her spacious igloo with her two daughters, one of which is a mermaid, the other a unicorn. When she is not writing, she is riding her moose and wrestling with her polar bear. Due to the demand of her books, she was forced to train her hamsters to guard her home, as she typed out what the crazy voices in her head demanded. She's an avid supporter of World Wildlife Fund and makes an effort to involve herself as well as her family in fundraising campaigns for various charities. Melissa has an Employment Counsellor Diploma from Fleming College, but she prefers writing stories over resumes. Presently, she has eleven books published in a variety of genres, which include Poetry, and Historical and Contemporary Romance.

ABOUT DAVID S. SCOTT

David S. Scott is a best selling author of erotica and erotic romance novels. After finishing his debut novels, *Deep in You* and its sequel *Deeper in You*, as well as *Santa's Son* and *Igniting Passions,* he is moving on to several other projects, including an erotic paranormal tentatively titled *Obsidian Angel.* He is in his mid-thirties and happily married, and has a bit of a wicked sense of humor. When not writing, David can be found reading a variety of genres or playing "nerd games" like Dungeons and Dragons with his friends.